Matil

The Children of the Great King

SALZWASSER
VERLAG

Matilda Horsburg

The Children of the Great King

Reprint of the original, first published in 1865.

1st Edition 2022 | ISBN: 978-3-75258-986-3

Verlag (Publisher): Salzwasser Verlag GmbH, Zeilweg 44, 60439 Frankfurt, Deutschland
Vertretungsberechtigt (Authorized to represent): E. Roepke, Zeilweg 44, 60439 Frankfurt, Deutschland
Druck (Print): Books on Demand GmbH, In de Tarpen 42, 22848 Norderstedt, Deutschland

THE CHILDREN

OF

THE GREAT KING.

A TALE OF THE CRIMEAN WAR.

BY M. H.

EDINBURGH

MDCCCLXV.

'What poor despised company
  Of travellers are these,
That walk in yonder narrow way,
  Along that rugged maze?

'Ah, these are of a royal line,
  All children of a King,
Heirs of immortal crowns divine,
  And, lo! for joy they sing.'

CHAPTER I.

'The Lord is a great King.'—Ps. xlvii. 2.

'There is a family on earth
Whose Father fills a throne;
But, though a seed of heavenly birth,
To men they're little known.
But 'tis the King who reigns above
That claims them for His own;
The favoured objects of His love,
And destined to a throne.'

THE spring months of the year 1854 were already passing away when our story commences.

Dark lowered the clouds in the political sky of many nations of the earth at that time; wars and rumours of wars prevailed on all sides. Russia had begun an unjust attack on Turkey, the provoking cause of the war being the contested possession of the holy places in the city of Jerusalem by the Greek and Latin Churches, in which contest the Turks had taken part against the Russians. Strange, indeed, that the birthplace and sepulchre of the

Prince of Peace should be made the excuse for all the horrors attendant on war!

Not unmoved had Britain's sons watched the rise and progress of the war. Ever averse to injustice and oppression, they saw with growing indignation their former ally, the Emperor of Russia, carrying on such an unequal unjust strife; so, after finding expostulation vain, they resolved to haste to the rescue of the oppressed people, though foreigners and of an adverse faith. Heavy fell the blow on many a British home, when the news spread, that, after a long season of peaceful rest, the nation's sword was once more to be unsheathed, and her sons to go forth, strong in the power of the Lord of hosts, to set the oppressed ones free.

Heartrending partings were taking place over all the land; high and low alike—in the lordly dwellings of the peer and the noble of the land, and the lowly cottage of the peasant of the soil. Wives, mothers, sisters, were shedding burning tears as they parted from dearly-loved ones they might see no more on earth. Alas! how many noble ones who went bravely, eagerly forth at the call of duty, returned no more! Winter winds and summer sunshine have passed over their graves in the far distant country many times since then; but their memory lives not only in the hearts of those who loved them, but in the remembrance of a nation; and their names stand proudly out, emblazoned already in historic records.

Mingled, indeed, were the feelings with which Colonel Percy heard the news that his regiment was ordered to Varna, from thence to proceed at further orders to the seat of war. Soldier-like, he was ever ready at the call of Queen and country for active service. In more than one hard-fought battle in India had he borne a conspicuous part; and all who knew him declared that no finer specimen of a brave, noble-hearted British officer could be found than Colonel Percy, of the gallant —— regiment.

Yet, when the order came, his thoughts instantly turned to his children, and for the first time he felt that the obeying it cost him a severe pang. Often before had he been separated from them, but then he left them in the care of the best of mothers. Now their home must be with comparative strangers, for the gentle mother was at rest in the Land where partings are no more. Only two short months had passed since father and children had mourned that heavy loss; and with the sore wound still fresh, the bitter grief yet keen as ever, no wonder that the father, brave soldier though he was, shrunk both for himself and children from the pain of a fresh, perhaps a life-long parting.

But not long were such feelings allowed to sway his well-disciplined heart. The tenderest, the most allowable of emotions, must yield to duty. Faithful servant of an earthly sovereign, to whom he had sworn fealty, and in whose defence, and in obedience to whose commands, he was ever ready to draw the sword, and, if need be, die on the battle-field, he never forgot he was none the less a servant of the great King, who is God over all; a good soldier of the Lord Jesus Christ, willing and ready in His cause to endure hardness, and uphold His banner against all foes.

His duty once plainly seen, and aid invoked where it is never invoked in vain, all arrangements were quickly made, for time pressed; and the father broke the news as gently as he could to his two motherless children. Most he feared for his gentle girl, his loving little Ada.

There they stood, the brother and sister; Claude (a fine bold boy, with the brown hair and flashing black eyes of his father) with his arm thrown caressingly round his sister, who, although little more than a year his junior, looked much younger than he, her fairy-like figure and her light golden hair falling in long curls round her almost to the waist, giving her a child-like appearance, which made one guess her younger than her real age, which was twelve years.

In silence the children listened as their father spoke, the full meaning of his words scarcely falling on them at first; but when all became plain, when they realized that the parting was at hand, that their home was to be with a stranger uncle in Devonshire, that their so loved father was going far away to battle, perhaps to death,—then it seemed as if a dark cloud came down over them, and shut out all the sunshine from their lives. 'Mamma dead, and papa leaving us,' were the first words Ada uttered, and, throwing herself into her father's arms, she wept the unrestrained tears of childhood.

Colonel Percy let her weep on, though every tear sent a pang to his heart. He tried not to stop her; he thought it best to let her grief have relief thus. Quietly, tenderly he held her, glancing only now and then at his boy, who stood, with eyes full of tears, but they fell not; a strong will kept them back, the flushed cheek and the firm-set lips showing how great was the effort.

Suddenly the door opened; the Colonel was required in another room on pressing business; he put down his child, and went at once. Claude went up to his sister, and, bending over her, said, 'Ada, darling Ada, don't cry so; papa must go, even if he wished ever so much to stay. A soldier would never draw back in the hour of danger; and, Ada, if you give way so, it will make it harder for him to go, and you would not like that, dear? Don't you remember how mamma never cried when papa went away, never before him—only after—yes, after, she cried bitterly; but one day she told me that she kept back her tears for papa's sake, to make it easier for him to go.'

At these words Ada sat up and dried her tears. The words had sunk deep, and, sensitive as she was, she possessed a resolute strength of purpose, which would develop itself quickly when called into exercise. Her woman-nature came to her aid; she would quiet herself for her father's sake, keep back her own grief to lessen his, and henceforth shed her tears in secret, seen only by Him to whom all places are open, to whom darkness and light are both alike.

Poor little Ada! having learned such a lesson, thou art a child no longer: the dawn of womanhood is breaking around thee; and, through sorer trials and more bitter grief, thou wilt learn to suffer and be strong, thy earthly reward the pure joy of unselfish love!

The evening before the departure had come, father and children sat talking together.

'Papa,' said Claude, 'I am thirteen and more already; in less than four years I shall be in the army, and fight by your side. Oh, papa, I wish I could go now, it is such a noble thing to be a soldier, to fight, and conquer of course; British soldiers always do that; and then the taking towns by storm, and feeling all the time we are fighting in defence of our country, and as faithful subjects of our Queen. I do so wish I were a little older, that I could be a soldier now.'

Colonel Percy looked at the boy's bright animated face, and felt a pleasure in the thought that no coward spirit was in his breast. Faults he had—a hasty temper, sometimes an impatience of reproof; but his nature was brave, truthful, and loving, and the father fondly hoped that, by the grace of God, his boy was being led into the right way, and was seeking, earnestly seeking, to overcome his faults. 'A soldier now, Claude! Yes, you may be so. Indeed I trust you are so, and for that matter, my little Ada too.'

'How, papa, what do you mean?' said both children in a breath.

Colonel Percy paused a moment; then laying his hand on his boy's shoulder, said gravely, 'Yes, Claude, a good soldier of the Lord Jesus Christ, fighting the good fight of faith.'

The boy pressed closer to his father. 'Papa, that is a very hard battle to fight, and we are not sure of being conquerors there. Often and often I begin the fight, and fall before the enemy.'

'How about the armour, Claude—the shield of faith, the sword of the Spirit? When the enemy comes, do you use these against him? What would you say of me, if I rushed to the battle-field unarmed, and then fell, and complained that my enemy was too powerful for me?'

'Oh, papa, you would never be so foolish; of course you would go prepared to fight.'

'Well, my children, never go out to the daily battle-field of life without the shield of faith, which is kept bright by prayer, and the sword of the Spirit, which is the Word of God. Have that daily hidden in your heart; and when Satan tempts you to do wrong, resist him; answer him as the Captain of our salvation did when he tempted Him: "It is written."'

Claude sighed. 'I could be very brave in an earthly battle-field, but a sad coward, I fear, in the one you speak of. I could fight against flesh and blood; but I so often fall under the rulers of the darkness,—I cannot stand against the wiles of the evil one.'

Never before had the boy spoken so openly of his feelings to his father, though for long Colonel Percy had seen the struggle, the endeavour to do the right thing, which was going on in his breast, and for which he had thanked God; now it seemed as if he were permitted to see the stumbling-block which was hindering his boy's growth in grace, that ere he left him he might be enabled to remove it. It was one easily seen—one, alas, which many souls have fallen against, and never risen again—self-righteousness; striving to overcome the great enemy of souls in our own strength, instead of going to Him who will impart to us His own.

'You say you cannot stand against the wiles of the evil one, Claude; no more you can in your own strength, but you can do all things through Christ strengthening you. You can, through Him, be more than conqueror; you can be strong in the Lord, and in the power of His might. Ask for that strength daily, and you will be enabled to do exploits more worthy far of renown than any earthly ones. What says the wise king, inspired by the Holy Spirit? "He that is slow to anger is better than the mighty, and he that ruleth his spirit than he that taketh a city."'

Claude's only answer was a pressure of his father's hand, and a whispered 'I see it, papa; I see what I should do.'

Then they spoke of the parting; Ada, with a full heart, not saying much, only keeping very close to her father's side, and silently taking in his every word; long, long to be remembered when her home was with strangers, and he was in the far-off battle-field.

Ere they parted, Colonel Percy put into the hands of each of the children a new Bible. 'Study it well,' he said, 'with prayer; consult it in all difficulties; follow its directions as minutely as a soldier does his marching orders. It is God's will, which points out every step you should take in the way to heaven, and warns you of all the dangerous places. Remember that God is King of kings, and a king demands obedience to his commands. Dear children, I leave you to His care. I have no greater wish for you than that you should be "Children of the Great King, the King of Glory."

They knelt in prayer, and sought the help and guidance of God the Father, God the Son, and God the Holy Ghost; and after a long loving embrace, the children were sent to rest, as for them also a long journey was in store on the morrow.

CHAPTER II.

'In a dream, in a vision of the night, when deep sleep falleth upon men, in slumberings upon the bed; then God openeth the ears of men, and sealeth their instruction.'—JOB xxxiii. 15, 16.

'REST,' thought Ada, and smiled at the thought; 'no rest for me to-night, when to-morrow is the day of papa's departure.' And her heart throbbed, and the burning tears fell fast enough as she lay down in the bed over which a mother had so often bent to bless her, and give the sweet good night; and the child longed to know if the spirit of her mother could see her now, could know that papa was going away, that Claude and she were henceforth for long, so long, to live with strangers.

Then she wondered if the Great King, who sees all His children, and loveth and careth for them, would go with Claude and her to their new home, and yet accompany and protect their father in the dangers of a foreign land; and something seemed to whisper, 'Yes! I will. Under the shadows of my wings I will keep you all till you meet again. I will never leave thee, nor forsake thee.' And, with the words sounding in her ears, she fell asleep, and slept the quiet sleep of childhood.

Not hers yet to know the grief which gnaws the heart, and banishes, effectually banishes, sleep from the eyes. Long, long may it be ere she knows that grief experienced only by those of riper years, caused often, or sorely increased, by the want of that child-like confidence in the sure guidance of the Father in heaven.

Quietly the child slept on, yet, through her sleep, her father's conversation and her last waking thoughts mingled with her dreams. She saw before her a steep road, tangled with thorns, and encumbered with large stones, over which she stumbled as she tried to force her way on to a splendid house she saw in the far distance. Over the gate which led to it, shone a bright light, brighter far than the sun; but its rays only cast a feeble glimmer on the path where the child walked, by reason of the thick trees which met overhead, and made all so dark, that, save when now and then they stood more apart, she could not even catch a glimpse of the beautiful house.

Torn with the thorns, and hurt with the stones, she sat down disconsolate, when suddenly in front of her she saw a glorious figure, clad in garments of pure white, and encircled by an unearthly light; he smiled on her, and, taking her by the hand, he led her gently on. At his presence the thorns disappeared; and if here and there the large stones still lay, the child fell not, for her guide carried her over them all. As they went on, now and then strange wild-looking creatures came out of the wood, as if they sought to carry off the child; but the moment they caught sight of her guide, they fled, leaving her unmolested.

Quite close she kept to his side, though sometimes, through very fear, she would have dropped her grasp of his hand; but at such moments she felt his hold of her was a strong one, and she knew that in that fact her safety lay.

Suddenly she saw Claude walking with them, held also firm by the other hand of the guide. Timidly Ada raised her eyes to the face of her conductor. 'Where will you lead us to?' she asked.

Kindly he looked at her, love sparkling in his eyes. 'Yonder,' he said, pointing out the shining house in the far distance, 'to the palace of the Great King.'

'Oh, how good!' exclaimed both children; 'but will it be long ere we reach it?'

'That I may not tell you; the length of the journey depends on the will of the King. But fear not, short or long, under my guidance you shall reach it safe at last.'

'And you,' said Ada, 'who are you?'

At the words, a halo of glory encircled his head; and there, written in letters of gold, she read the words, 'The Son of the Great King, the Prince of Peace.'

Something, she scarce knew what, roused her from her dream. She looked up; the early summer sun was already darting its rays through the opening of the shutters, telling that another day was begun. Peace seemed to rest in the heart of the child; 'twas as if, by visions of the night, the King of kings had commissioned His angels to minister comfort to the motherless girl.

Little she knew, that whilst she lay wrapped in slumber, a father's farewell kiss had been imprinted on her forehead, a father's blessing pronounced over her head, and that already Colonel Percy was on his way to the post of duty. He had meant to awake her as he had done Claude; but her calm, peaceful face, though on the long lashes still hung some of the tears shed ere she fell asleep, determined him to spare her the pain of parting. And so he let her sleep on, and left her—left her in the keeping of One who, he knew, would fail her not—the safe keeping of the Great King.

CHAPTER III.

'Green the land is, where my daily steps in jocund child-
hood played,
Dimpled close with hill and valley, dappled very close with
shade;
Summer, snow of apple blossoms running up from glade
to glade.'

'FRANCES, don't you wish they would come before the sun sets? it will be so dismal for them to arrive amongst strangers, and at a strange place, in the dark.'

The words were spoken by a pale, delicate-like boy of nine years old, with large dreamy blue eyes, who stood looking out of the window in a country house in Devonshire, eagerly waiting the appearance of some expected guests. His question was addressed to a girl who sat near him, ostensibly occupied with a book, but in reality glancing out of the window every now and then as eagerly as her brother, for such he was, though in the outward appearance of the two there was as marked a difference as in their inward dispositions. No look of dreaminess about the girl's dark eye and bold countenance, and no sentimentality in either the words or tone with which she answered his query.

'Not I, Arthur; I don't care the least bit whether it is light or dark when they come, nor indeed whether they come at all or not. I don't believe I will like them; stupid, moping things, I daresay. I'm sure there will be no fun. Now, Arthur, don't open your eyes so wide at me, and look so horrified. Of course I remember all papa and mamma said to us about being kind to them, and all that; and I don't wish them any harm, only 'tis horrid to be put out of one's way, and—'

'Oh, Frances!' said the boy, 'how you do talk; and you know they have no home of their own now. Their mother is dead, and their papa away, perhaps to battle. I do hope they will come while that beautiful sun is pouring its light like gold through those green leaves, and lighting up those trees in the orchard. Our home is so lovely to-night: I know they will love it if they see it so.'

The child stood gazing at the peaceful scene before him, wrapt in delight. His sister looked at him, half in disdain, half in wonder. Little had she in common with his sensitive, ardent nature; but in her own way she dearly loved her brother, and to strangers was often heard to boast of Arthur's cleverness and his old-world remarks. The window was open, the sweet scent of blossom and flowers filled the room; the rustle of leaves, fanned by the gentle breeze, and the melodious carolling of the birds, were for long the only sounds that reached the ear.

Presently, however, carriage-wheels were heard in the distance, and a gentleman's voice called, 'Frances! Arthur! come down; your cousins are coming!'

A few minutes afterwards, and Claude and Ada Percy received a warm welcome from their uncle and aunt and young cousins, and were soon comfortably ensconced in their new home; and ere the twilight had changed into darkness, wearied out with the fatigues of the day, both children were fast asleep, watched over and kept from evil by the Keeper of Israel, who slumbereth not nor sleepeth.

Whilst they rest, we will give a short sketch of the people amongst whom their life was for a while to be spent.

Mr Willoughby, the eldest brother of the Percys' dead mother, had for many years resided on his property in Devonshire, farming a large portion of it himself, not merely nominally, as many gentlemen farmers do, but actively and incessantly directing and superintending everything; acting, in short, as his own steward. He was a man of no ordinary abilities, and of no mean scholarly attainments. His natural tastes were refined, and his little Arthur's intense love of the beautiful, as well as his feeling heart and gentle manners, were all inherited from his father.

In many respects father and son were much alike, —the same ardent disposition, the same deep powers of loving, the same disposition to look in on their own minds and analyze their most secret thoughts. In the boy, delicate from his birth, this tendency was beginning to be a hurtful one, leading him to dwell too much on himself, and, young as he was, tempting him to an habitual dreaminess. Such a tendency had, in Mr Willoughby's case, been early checked by a public school education, and in later years by constant occupation, and a strong will (stronger than Arthur would ever have) enabled him to overcome any inherent inclination to mere idle dreaming; indeed, the great feature of his character was that of power. All in his household and neighbourhood acknowledged it, and almost unconsciously yielded to his sway.

The only one who rebelled against it was his eldest child, Frances, a bold reckless girl of thirteen, not really bad, but possessing no depth of feeling. She was utterly careless of hurting the feelings of others; and after having spent some months with two cousins older than herself, who were aiming at attaining the unenviable character of fast young ladies, she had taken to imitate them, and by adopting, when away from the restraint of her parents or governess, their manners and phrases, was fast making herself disliked by all who knew her.

Mrs Willoughby was a kind, motherly person, never idle, occupied constantly either in or out of doors; in the morning hours never to be met without a large bunch of keys in her hands; in the afternoon busy receiving callers or returning visits; frequent in her visits to the nursery to see a sweet little curly-headed girl of two years old, little Minnie, the pet of the family; and to the school-room, to see how Frances and Arthur were getting on with their governess, Miss Manley. An active, bustling lady was Mrs Willoughby, inclined slightly to hold her husband's poetical tastes and feelings in disdain, and entirely ignorant of the meaning or the possibility of time hanging heavy on the hands of any one. From her the motherless children would receive all kindness and full justice. The only felt want (and oh what a want it is!) would be a lack of sympathy; the free outpouring of their hearts must now be made to God alone, the great Sympathizer.

CHAPTER IV.

'Fear thou not; for I am with thee: be not dismayed; for I am thy God: I will help thee; yea, I will uphold thee with the right hand of My righteousness.' — Isa. xli. 10.

SOME weeks had passed since the Percys arrived at their Devonshire home, and they were gradually settling down into the quiet routine of their new life. Claude, as had been arranged by his father, boarded with a clergyman in the immediate neighbourhood, only residing in his uncle's house from Saturday till Monday.

Ada was at once attracted by the gentle, winning manners of little Arthur. In play-hours they were always seen together, in rainy days poring over some favourite book; or when, accompanied by Frances and Miss Manley, they took their daily walk, it was Arthur who pointed out the beautiful views and told the quaint traditions of many a spot, which he had learned from his old nurse, or had picked up from the old-fashioned books he delighted to read.

Many a taunt Ada had to bear from Frances, for taking up, as she termed it, with such a child as Arthur; but Ada bore them quietly. Between Frances and herself she felt there was nothing in common, and not to quarrel with her was her greatest desire. 'Bear and forbear, my child,' had been her dead mother's favourite advice, and on it Ada strove to act; but, with one so provoking as Frances, it was not easy to do so, and ere long Ada saw plainly that her path was becoming a steep one, strewn with thorns—small ones, perhaps, but sharp in wounding.

How often in life we find that the thorns or trials that are so ill to bear, so sharp and piercing, are little ones—things that even to ourselves we blush to own hurt us at all. So was it with Ada. Real unkindness, sharp words from any one, she could have borne better than the constant mocking, real or feigned, of her cousin, and the petty tricks which were played off upon her.

The girls slept in rooms next to each other, and dearly did Ada prize the early morning hour, when she could study in quiet, in the Bible her father had given her, the will of the Great King. One morning, as she sat thus occupied, forgetting all petty annoyances in reading of the life and sufferings of our Saviour, Frances burst in. 'What are you about, Ada?—reading the Bible! What in the world do you do that for? 'tis not Sunday, and you'll hear papa read a chapter at prayer-time, you know. Put that away now, and come out for a while to the garden. I must have you, 'tis so early, and I want to wash my face in the dew : come, quick.'

In vain Ada said she would not, she preferred to stay and read ; 'And besides, Frances, did not Miss Manley tell us the other day that we were not to go out again in the morning so early ?'

'Bother Miss Manley ; who cares what she says ?' was the impetuous answer. 'Besides, she is in bed fast asleep, and would never see us or know a word about it. Come away, and don't be a goose.'

At first Ada had hesitated, she dreaded so to oppose her cousin ; but now the holy words she had been reading came to her help, and she boldly answered, 'No, Frances, I shall not go ; we were forbidden to do so ; and if Miss Manley does not see us, the Great King does, and He has desired us to obey those that have the rule over us.'

'What do you mean, Ada ? Who is the great king, and how could he see us ? Kings have something else to do than watch the pranks of girls like you and me.' But Ada's only answer was, pointing to a verse in the Bible she held, 'The eyes of the Lord are in every place, beholding the evil and the good.' 'He is the Great King,' she whispered ; 'I must obey His commands.'

'Absurd, Ada, as if He cared about a little thing

like this; I believe it is all pretence your speaking that way, you just do it to make me angry. If Arthur had asked you, you would have done it, and no word about right or wrong.' And so saying, she went away, slamming the door after her.

Poor Ada, she knew she had done right, but she felt disconsolate and frightened for the consequences of her cousin's anger. Oh for some one to help and guide her now! Papa away, and even Claude, she drooped her head, and the bright morning sun shone on her eyes wet with tears. Turning the leaves of her Bible, she saw the words, 'Fear not, I will hold thee by the right hand, I will help thee.'

Suddenly she remembered her dream; the guide who had held her hand and led her over all difficulties, was the Son of the Great King, the Lord Jesus. With His help she would bear all things; and, kneeling down, she sought earnestly that He would be true to His promise, and hold her fast, enabling her to do His will. Can we doubt that her prayer received a full answer? No; 'for this is the confidence that we have in Him, that if we ask anything according to His will, He heareth us.' And her prayer was in full accordance with the will of Him who hath said, 'Wilt thou not from henceforth say unto me, My Father, Thou art the guide of my youth?'

With a lighter heart she rose, and proceeded to the school-room. Miss Manley and Arthur greeted her kindly, but through the whole day Frances bestowed nothing but black looks on her; and when in one or two things Ada volunteered to help her, all the thanks she got was, 'Go away, I don't wish your help, nor your company either; saints are not in my line at all.'

Saint! Poor Ada, the rush of angry feelings called forth by her cousin's words, told her how far she was from meriting such a name. No, no; full of imperfection and sin she was, and knew herself to be; but her hand, feeble as it was, had knocked at the door of the throne of mercy, her heavenward pilgrimage was begun; and from the land of glory, angels and the spirits of the just made perfect—the great Cloud of Witnesses—stooped to watch the progress in grace, slow it might be, but sure, of one of the children of the Great King.

CHAPTER V.

'Though sin, and death, and hell
Your heavenly march oppose,
Fear not, it shall be well,
God will confound your foes:
On Him depend, the fight renew.
As Gideon conquered, so shall you.'

THE parsonage where Claude was boarded was a pleasantly situated house, commanding a beautiful view of the sea, down to the very edge of which sloped thickly-wooded hills, whilst the beach was near enough to permit the boys on a half holiday to walk there, and amidst the rocks and caverns search out the exquisitely beautiful zoophytes, and the many varieties of sea anemones, serpularia, and other creatures which there abound.

Bitterly Claude felt at first the leaving Ada alone amongst people whom she hardly knew; and even the little he had seen of Frances made him fear that his little sister would in many ways be sorely tried by her. But Ada had never forgotten the lesson of unselfishness which Claude himself had taught her on the evening their father had first told of his intended departure ; and though she would have liked to have told him of the many petty trials she had to bear, she did not do so, knowing how he would vex himself about it.

So, when the Saturdays came round, she always contrived to have a smiling face to welcome her brother, eagerly listening to all his stories of his school life, reading over and over with him the letters received during the week from their father, telling him how kind uncle and aunt were, retailing some of Arthur's clever sayings and quaint remarks, and laughing over little Minnie's droll attempts at speaking ; and as Claude listened to her, he felt sure his idea about her being annoyed by Frances must have been a wrong one, and he returned to school pleased that Ada was so happy.

Well, older and wiser than he have been deceived in like manner many and many a time ; and it is best it should be so. It is not well to vex even those of whose sympathy we are surest, with all our difficulties and little thorns. There are burdens which, as far as man is concerned, 'tis best to bear alone ; but none, great or small, which we may not roll on the Lord.

Claude's master, Mr Marshman, was loved by all who knew him. Earnest alike in his clerical work and in the responsible one of education which he had undertaken, he was well qualified to lead such a boy as Claude. Strict in discipline, but yet unfailing in love and true sympathy, the right-minded boys felt a rebuke from him or a displeased look the greatest of punishments; and ere long Claude felt he could speak to him, and seek his advice as he had done that of his father.

Hitherto Claude had mixed little, too little, with other boys, and he felt that his great difficulties lay with them. Some amongst them there were wanting in that sense of honour and truth on which Claude prided himself; and from these he shrank with abhorrence, forgetting that his own faults, though of a different kind, were conspicuous enough.

In especial, he was tried by one boy, a relation of his Aunt Willoughby's, of the name of Whitmore. He was about a year younger than himself, one who thought little of hiding a fault by a falsehood, or shifting blame off his own shoulders on that of others. Once or twice had Claude detected him in doing so, and his loud protestations had called down his indignation on him as a meddling fool.

Claude, full of disgust at such meanness, took credit to himself for having given his opinion of him so forcibly. 'I won't be a partaker of other people's sins,' he said, 'and see them going on like that, without letting them know how wicked and mean it is. I declare, if it were not I could not bear to be a tell-tale, I would let Mr Marshman know.'

Softly, softly, Claude! he that would pull the mote out of his brother's eye, must first have plucked the beam out of his own. It is well, it is right to warn our companions of the errors of their ways, but remember it becometh sinful beings like ourselves to speak the truth IN LOVE. When we feel we can do that, then, but not till then, are we fit to reprove the faults of others. In his first indignation at the sins of Charlie Whitmore, Claude was forgetting to watch against his own; and not until sent to his room for an outburst of passion, did he see clearly that his self-righteous spirit was a device of his great enemy to cause him to fall. Defeated again in the spiritual battle-field, and that when he was feeling so sure of victory, no wonder he was abashed. But rejoice not over him, thou enemy of souls! though he has fallen, he shall rise again, humbled by the fall, but better able to cope with thee; for, having learned his own weakness, he has sought more strength from the strong One, against whose power thou art feeble indeed!

Kindly and forcibly Mr Marshman reasoned with the boy on the evil of thus giving way to passion, reminding him of the Scripture declaration, that 'he that hath no rule over his spirit, is like a city that is broken down and without walls.' 'And,' said he, 'you know well enough, Claude, how easily the enemy can rush into and take possession of a city which they find thus unprotected.'

Claude owned his fault, and from that time became more watchful, more fearful of falling; and remembering his father's advice, he sought more earnestly the help of the Great King.

Anxiously did Mr Marshman watch him; he was attracted by the open, ingenuous character of the boy, and felt that, rightly used, his example might prove a blessing to the other boys. At the same time, he was fully alive to his failings, and determined, as far as he could, and by the help of God, to eradicate them. He noticed at once the bad feeling which had sprung up between Claude and Whitmore, and felt it his duty to put a stop to it, though for a while he was puzzled as to what would be the best means of doing so.

An opportunity soon occurred. On one occasion Charlie Whitmore had been detected in falsehood by Mr Marshman, and severely punished. 'Serve him right,' was the feeling amongst the other boys, who all disliked Whitmore. That evening Claude found Mr Marshman sitting alone, looking tired and vexed. He had gone into the room looking for a book he had left, and seeing Mr Marshman sitting, turned at once, fearing to disturb him. Somewhat to his surprise, he heard himself called back, and desired to sit down, as Mr Marshman wished to speak to him.

'There is not much love between you and Charlie Whitmore, Claude, I see. How is that?'

'Love! no indeed, sir, there's precious little of that between us; he hates me, and—and'—as he spoke he stammered,—'I suppose I am not much better. I don't like him, that is certain: he would do anything to spite me; but indeed, sir, I would rather not say anything more about him, for I always feel angry when I even think of him.'

'Then, in fact,' said Mr Marshman, 'you count him your enemy?'

'Pretty near that, sir,' replied Claude.

'Well, Claude, that being the case, what is your duty concerning him? What is the command of the Great King? Read here,' taking up the Bible, '"I say unto you, Love your enemies, do good to them that hate you, and pray for them which despitefully use you."'

The boy flushed scarlet as he read. 'Well, Claude, is it not your desire to obey the King's will in all things?'

'Yes, sir, I do wish, but I never thought of it as applying to Whitmore and me. *Some* enemies, it may mean.'

Mr Marshman interrupted him:

'Nay, Claude, the verse makes no exception; it

does not say, Love all your enemies except young Whitmore?'

'No, sir, of course, but it would be hard to do. I don't think I could.'

'Claude, do you think the Lord ever commands His people to do anything which it is impossible for them to do,—ever lays upon them burdens which He will not help them to bear, if they ask Him? It is Satan who bids us hate our enemies; and, my boy, never forget, that, whatever you may profess, in reality "ye are the servants of him whom ye obey." And, Claude, I believe if you try to love Charlie Whitmore, it will prove not only a blessing to yourself, but to him also. I believe, if anything will do him good, it will be done by love. Poor boy, I pity him, for his advantages have been few: his father is a busy merchant, always too occupied to devote time to his children; and he never knew a mother's care or love. She died when he was born, so the boy has grown up neglected; none have sought to lead him in the right way. He fears me too much; and I, sorely against my will, have had to punish him, for example's sake, too often to have gained much ground with him. I believe if a boy of his own age could gain his love and confidence, it might be the saving of him. Claude, to you may belong the honour, the blessing, of leading him to the Great King. Will you try?'

For one moment Claude hesitated, then said in a tone of emotion, 'God helping me, I will, sir.'

From that day Claude held no longer aloof from Charlie Whitmore, but sought by all means to win his confidence, not by abetting in the smallest degree his faults, but by kindness striving to remove the bad feeling which had sprung up between them. Was Whitmore in difficulty over his Greek or Latin? Claude offered his aid. At first it was repelled; but by degrees, seeing the offer was made in earnest, it was accepted; with wonder, it is true, why Percy should concern himself about him.

At first, it must be acknowledged, the effort was a great one to Claude. To lay aside a prejudice, and that a well-grounded one, is easy neither for young nor old; and but for the boy's desire to do right, to overcome his wrong feelings, and obey the commands of the heavenly King, he would have given up the task as hopeless. But the victory over himself was gained, and as time passed on he had his reward; for, touched by his kindness, the neglected boy became warmly attached to him; and seeing Claude's straightforward, truthful behaviour, learned at least to respect these qualities in him, and through fear of incurring his displeasure, strove against deceitful ways. The motive at first was not the right one, but nevertheless it was a step in the right direction; and Claude despaired not, that ere long he would seek to do right from a higher motive, even out of love to the Great King. With pleasure Mr Marshman watched the two boys, and saw how each in their different ways were improving.

Knowing well how powerful is the force of example, Claude was daily, in the strength of the Lord, subduing his hasty temper. Many a sore struggle it cost him. Often in the middle of a game, when tempted by some hasty word to return an angry, passionate reply, he gulped it down, remembering that by giving way to temper he was not only sinning against the Master he served, but casting a stumbling-block in the way of one who, though in much weakness, was yet, he hoped, really beginning to enter on the path of life.

Was the victory thus obtained over himself a small one? Answer me, school-boys! When angry passions are up, and hard words and names are hurled at each other, is it easy to bear them, and retort not; easy to stand the very chaffing provoked by silence? Or, say, is not he who can bear such an attack steadily and unflinchingly, a greater hero than he who stands undismayed whilst the enemy's balls are flying over his head?

Yet to himself it seemed as if he were making but little progress; so many wrong feelings to be daily resisted, so many enemies to be slain. One overcome, another arose; but the eye of the Great Captain of his salvation was on the boy, and He noted that step by step he was advancing ; fighting his way, it is true, inch by inch, but recognising more and more, that the arm which upheld him, the smile which encouraged, the love which allured him, were all from above, all proceeding from Him who is King of kings and Lord of lords.

CHAPTER VI.

'Lord, Thou hast won, at length I yield.
My heart, by mighty grace compelled,
Surrenders all to Thee.
Now, Lord, I would be Thine alone;
Come, take possession of Thine own,
For Thou hast set me free.
Released from Satan's hard commands,
See all my powers waiting stand
To be employed by Thee.'

ONE glorious August Sabbath afternoon, Ada and Arthur were sitting together in a small arbour in the garden.

Flowers of every kind, of the most beautiful hues and sweetest perfume, were around them. On their right-hand side stood the orchard, the trees laden with their fast-ripening fruit; on their left the large shrubbery, in which many of the rarest shrubs were to be seen. On each side of the bower were myrtles, growing to such a height that their branches mingled together till they formed a canopy; while intermixed with them, and presenting a beautiful contrast to their glossy dark-green leaves, were numbers of the exquisite *Devoniensis* roses. Close by played a fountain, its waters falling into a pure white marble basin.

A slight, very slight, haze had arisen, which tempered a little the burning heat of the sun, and yet rather increased than diminished the beauty around. Not a breath stirred the trees; all nature seemed hushed; the chirp of the birds, the hum of some bees as they flew home to their hives laden with spoil, and the gentle splash, splash, of the water, were the only sounds that broke the silence.

Both children sat gazing at the sights around them, enraptured with their beauty, almost fearing to speak, lest at the sound of their words the whole should vanish as in a tale of fairy land.

Arthur was the first to break the silence. 'Ada, is it not lovely? and all, all, as you say, the workmanship of the Great King! How very great He must be! And, Ada, do you know, I can't help being so glad to think He must love what is beautiful, or He never would have made the earth so fair.' The boy raised his eyes to heaven, as if he found in this thought a bond of union between the Creator and himself. 'Ada, speak! are not you sure He does?'

'Oh, yes, I know it, Arthur; see here!' she said, opening the Bible she held in her hand; 'He tells us so in His word. After He had created the world, He looked at it, and behold it was very good; and

He loves to look on it still. The Psalmist says, "The Lord rejoiceth in His works;" and, Arthur, look at this verse in the fourth chapter of Revelation; papa showed it to Claude and me one day. After the four and twenty elders have cast their crowns before the throne of Jesus, they sing, "Thou art worthy, O Lord, to receive glory, and honour, and power: for Thou hast created all things, and for Thy pleasure they are and were created."'

'Yes, Ada, I like that: read it again. For His pleasure! Oh! that is so good. The Great King can see every place; so He can see this very spot, and rejoice in its beauty. He sees us too; and, oh! Ada, I don't do His will as I should; and, till you came, I never even used to think of Him at all, nor of Jesus the Son of the Great King. Is He King as well as His Father?'

'Yes,' answered Ada, 'I asked papa that one day, and he told me He was equal in glory; and so is the Holy Ghost, who dwells in the hearts of those who love Him, and makes them holy.'

Arthur sat a few minutes lost in thought; then said, 'Ada, tell me again about your dream about the guide and the king's palace.' Ada told him all. When she ceased, his face was a-glow with joy: 'I see it so clearly now; yes, your guide must have been the kind Jesus, who when He was on earth loved the children and blessed them. I do hope He will be my guide too, and hold me fast. But, Ada, do you know I often think my journey will be a short one. I heard a lady, who was calling on mamma the other day, say to a friend who was with her, "That boy is not long for this world." Of course she did not know that I heard her. For a moment I could not bear the thought; but I remembered your dream, and then I felt so glad to think that I would, perhaps with Jesus as my guide, soon reach the palace of the Great King.'

A rustling of leaves at their back startled the children, and made them look round, just as Mr Willoughby entered the bower, and, sitting down, drew his boy lovingly to his side. Attracted by their voices, he had been drawn to the bower, and had overheard with some surprise their conversation. He had meant to go away without disturbing them; but Arthur's last words had sent a thrill through him, and awoke a dread, which for some time he had overcome—the fearful dread that his loved only son would be early taken away. Not one word could he at first say; he only pressed a kiss on the boy's forehead, and held him as if to guard him from some threatening danger.

Arthur was accustomed to his father's caresses, and did not appear to think them anything remarkable in the present instance; but Ada saw at once how it was, and longed to say a word to comfort her uncle. But just as she was beginning to say something, in the hope to make him forget Arthur's words, Claude came running up to them, and said that Miss Manley desired them to come in, as she wished to hear them say their Bible lesson before it was time to go to the evening church.

Mr Willoughby released Arthur, and desired him to go in with Claude, and tell Miss Manley that Ada would come presently. 'I wish to speak with her for a short time; but don't put off the Bible lesson for her, I will hear her's myself.' Both boys were somewhat astonished at their message; but went off at once, Claude expressing to Arthur his wonder how Ada would like to say her lesson to uncle.

'Oh! she won't be frightened a bit,' Arthur declared; 'don't you notice, Claude, when Ada says or reads anything out of the Bible, she seems always as if she were standing in the very presence of the Great King, and forgets all about any one in the room?'

Yes, Claude knew quite well the sort of look Ada had then, and said that Arthur was right, and she would have no fear.

As soon as the boys were out of hearing, Mr Willoughby said, 'Ada, tell me truly, is Arthur ill? does he complain? and if so, why have I not been told? I overheard your conversation, and made out that the boy thinks he is dying.'

'No, no, uncle, I don't think Arthur quite meant that; only you know he is never very strong, and the lady's remark has made an impression on him. You know he so often broods over a thing; and even when he spoke, I don't think he thought he was dying or ill now, only that perhaps his journey might not be so long as that of those who were stronger. Indeed, uncle, you must not vex yourself about what he said; I am sure neither aunt nor Miss Manley thinks he is ill.'

Mr Willoughby drew a long breath, as if relieved. 'Well, Ada, I hope you are right; he does not look worse, but we must rouse him, and not let him mope. Please God, he may be spared to us yet. And, now, come and tell me about the Great King; His words, you know, Ada, are for old as well as young. Let me see what is the Bible lesson for to-day.'

Ada turned it up. 'It is in the 21st chapter of St Luke, from the 25th verse to the 37th. It is about the second coming of Jesus, the Son of the Great King, who shall come in a cloud with power and great glory.' Solemnly and distinctly Ada repeated the passage, so full of instruction and warning.

Long after she had finished, and at her uncle's bidding had gone in to Miss Manley, he sat still, the words she had spoken echoing in his ears; and almost unconsciously he repeated over and over the pointed warning, 'Take heed to yourself, lest at any time your hearts be overcharged with the cares of this life, and so that day come upon you unawares.' As vividly as if a voice from heaven had called him by name, and delivered the words as a message sent to himself, did they now come home to his heart.

Mr Willoughby was not a man unmindful of the concerns of his soul, or without a certain degree of respect, nay, even love, for the Lord. When a young man, he had taken a warm interest in religious things, and still was ever ready with his money, and a good word, to help the cause of the Lord; but he knew nothing of real fellowship with the Father, Son, and Holy Spirit. His soul had never thirsted, as the true Christian does, for God, the living God; he had realized not a personal Saviour. He had once been partially advanced in the knowledge of these things; the light had broken so far, when he had come to a sudden stop, and the light, though not extinguished, had become clouded, neither clear nor dark; and why?

In the inmost depths of his soul the question was answered. The cares of this life had overcharged his heart; so much so, that, like the inn at Bethlehem, there was no place left for the Saviour to dwell there; and were Christ to appear that day, or death to call him to His presence, as a snare it would come upon him and find him unprepared. What, then, was he to do? how escape from the evil effects of the cares of this life? Ada's Bible, which he still retained in his hand, told him the only course to pursue for pardon of sin—to wash in the fountain of Jesus' shed blood, and for the future watch and pray. And there, in that lovely bower, amidst one of the sweetest scenes of the Creator's handiwork, an earnest child-like prayer for pardon and guidance rose to heaven, and was presented by the great Intercessor to the King; and a song of joy was heard from angels' lips, singing through the courts of heaven, that yet another soul was awakened from spiritual sleep, and was pressing on to the city of the Great King.

As Mr Willoughby walked with his wife and children that evening to the house of God, it seemed to him as if he had begun a new existence; every object in nature appeared clothed in new beauty; the very rays of the evening sun which fell in showers around, playing on hills and trees and corn-covered fields, and turning the graceful spire of the church to gold, reminded him of the glory before the Throne. The service of the sanctuary was precious to his soul, refreshing it as the falling dew. He noted how earnestly, how sweetly, the child-like voices of Claude, Ada, and his own Arthur chimed in when the evening hymn echoed through the little church.

'Glory to Thee, my God, this night,
For all the blessings of the light.
Keep me, oh! keep me, King of kings,
Under Thine own almighty wings!'

He realized for himself now the blessing of such a keeping. But many in that church knew it not; wise in the things of time, they lacked the children's simple faith. Now, just as in the days when Jesus dwelt on the earth, those things are often hid from the wise and prudent, and revealed unto babes. 'Even so, Father; for so it seemeth good in Thy sight.'

As they walked home in the subdued evening light, Arthur, who held his father's hand, pointed to a beautiful fleecy cloud (which lay cradled near the setting sun, 'a gleam of crimson tingeing its braided snow'), saying, 'Oh, papa, mamma, look how lovely!'

Both looked, at his request, and acknowledged its beauty; and Mr Willoughby, gazing at it as if penetrating into the depths beyond, answered, more his own thoughts than the child's, 'Yes, the very balancing of the clouds is the work of the Great King, who is perfect in knowledge.'

Mrs Willoughby looked at her husband, somewhat puzzled; but Arthur saw in his face the expression of the hidden joy which he had learnt to know, and only wondered he had never noticed papa have that look before. Little he dreamed, that the Lord of glory had made use of the words spoken by him and Ada to rouse from a spiritual torpor the soul of one so dear to them ; thus out of the mouths of babes perfecting His praise.

CHAPTER VII.

'Time passed on; but not with time
Did thoughts of Thee and Thine depart;
The lesson of forgetfulness
Was what I could not teach my heart.'

THE discipline in the school-room of Willoughby House, under the rule of Miss Manley, had never been of a strict description,—Frances and Arthur having been accustomed to do pretty much as they pleased; the boy studying, it is true, but only because he liked to do so, and when he was inclined for it; Frances doing so only in order to be able to answer the questions put to her when Mr and Mrs Willoughby made their weekly examination.

Miss Manley was a highly educated, gentle-minded Christian lady, but totally unfitted for enforcing her authority as a governess, on any child inclined to dispute it, by her want of firmness. Conscientiously desirous of performing her duty, Frances's carelessness and Arthur's fits of absent dreaminess tried her sorely, whilst her shrinking disposition made her averse to complain to Mrs Willoughby.

Ada's presence from the first proved an immense advantage; her steady application to her lessons, and her obedience to orders, were a great assistance to the governess. Abashed by her example, Frances (in spite of rallying her cousin on her quiet ways) gave up some of her flightiness, and applied herself to her books more steadily; whilst Arthur, at first stimulated by the sight of Ada's industry, and afterwards from higher motives, was now roused from his dreams, and exerted himself, not, as formerly, in learning those lessons only which pleased himself, but also in preparing those more distasteful to him.

With joy Miss Manley soon saw the simple, trusting faith which Ada possessed. Love to her Saviour God, and submission to His will, filled her own heart; but she was one of His hidden ones, whose timid temperament hindered her from speaking to others, as she often longed to do, of Him whom her soul loved. But her life spoke; and a widowed mother and young brother in her London home, knowing how much she had sacrificed for their sakes, never breathed her name without a blessing, never read her loving letters, filled as they were with the spirit of the Master she served, without having their thoughts raised heavenward, and feeling that the Lord was indeed an all-sufficient help to those who trusted in Him.

'Ada, don't you hate commonplace people?' asked Frances one day, as she and her cousin sat alone at work; 'people, you know, who just go on day by day, always doing the same thing, and yet not apparently disliking it, never caring much about anything, incapable of either liking or hating; just humdrum people, without an idea beyond the duty of the present hour, who can do nothing grand or heroic; people, in short, like Miss Manley, well enough in her way, but, as Letty Roscoe said (the week she spent here), as uninteresting as those stupid zoophytes that Arthur talks about, that are rooted to one spot, and belong half to the animal, half to the vegetable kingdom.'

Ada looked up, perfectly amazed at her curious way of talking. 'Oh, Frances, indeed Miss Manley is not at all commonplace. Think how clever she is; don't you remember uncle said the other day that he knew few ladies who had read so much and so thoughtfully as Miss Manley? As to her doing anything grand or heroic, I don't know exactly what you mean by that; I think it is a very grand thing to be able to do what is right, as she does, and she is always so kind and patient.'

'There now, Ada, that will do; I forgot you always sing Miss Manley's praises, and, as to her being patient, that is just the thing I dislike the most. If she were not that, if one could rouse her into a fury, I would like it ten times better than that martyr air she puts on, when I do all I can to provoke her. Yes, I would like to have a governess who was a heroine of some sort, and then, you know, I could respect her.'

A heroine! Well, Miss Manley would certainly have disdained any right to such a title; but there were some who, knowing the story of her life, thought her more worthy of the name than many who have earned it. Once, in the country town where Mr Manley was the wealthy flourishing banker, the favourite topic for a whole week was the approaching marriage of his only daughter to the second son of a gentleman of property in the neighbourhood, a young officer in the Queen's service. Some wondered that Mr Manley allowed his pretty daughter to make such a match, as the world said Captain Ainsworth possessed nothing save his pay, and pretty Mary Manley might at least have made a wealthier marriage. But instead of a marriage came death. From house to house sped the sad news, Mr Manley was dead; suddenly, very suddenly, from what cause it was scarcely known, only it was whispered he had been thrown into a fearful state of agitation by the receipt of a letter.

Reports spread; a panic was raised; a run on the bank feared; but confidence was restored by the open declaration of the Manleys' solicitor, that, though he grieved to say Mr Manley's own fortune had been completely lost through the failure of an unfortunate speculation, the bank was safe. His late friend, imprudent as he had been in thus venturing his own fortune, was not one to have tampered with the money entrusted to his care.

That the marriage was postponed was a matter of course; but as a few weeks passed on, rumour, with its busy tongue, said it was broken off, and, not content with stating facts, added as the cause, that, Mary Manley's fortune having disappeared, Captain Ainsworth's love had grown cold, and he had broken off the match.

But rumour in this matter, as in many others, spoke falsely. The marriage was broken off, but from no mercenary motives on Captain Ainsworth's part. Willingly would he have carried it out, and borne off his bride from the poverty which was now her lot; but Mary—how could she bear to leave her mother unprovided for, and her young brother also, who had just begun to study for a doctor? A small house in the suburbs of London, and L.80 a year, was all that was left to the widow and children, once accustomed to every comfort. Mary hesitated not, fondly as she loved Herbert Ainsworth; her love for him must be subordinated to her duty to her parent. She determined for some years to go as governess, and thus enable her brother to finish his course at college;

and then, but not till then, she felt, when he was able to provide for himself and his mother, that she might become the wife of Captain Ainsworth.

She told him her plans, but he was too indignant to hear her out, or listen to reason. If she had loved him as he did her, she would never have made such a proposal. What! put off their marriage till they were both old people? Not he, indeed; six months he would wait, out of respect to her father's memory, but not a day longer. He allow his Mary to go as a governess; never!

Calmly Mary stood her ground: too strongly her own wishes were identical with his; but she was a servant of the Great King, and she must do that which His law and her own conscience told her was right. Let the consequences be what they might, she saw the path she ought to pursue, and would not be turned aside. In vain she reminded Herbert that in four years he would only be twenty-seven, she scarce twenty-two; not so very old surely, and by that time Frank's college expenses would be over, and then she would feel free to marry.

But reasoning and remonstrances were alike in vain; and with a soreness of heart not to be described, she, taking off her ring of engagement, told Herbert that from henceforth he was free, but she must follow the path of duty. He listened to her in a passion too great for words; bowed coldly; thanked her for setting him free; and, without vouchsafing her another word, shook hands, and parted.

Not a heroine! Frances Willoughby, could you have seen Mary Manley in the night hours, for long weeks after that day, and have realized, even in the slightest degree, her mental agony, even you would ever after have ceased to look with contempt on your gentle governess, and allowed her sacrifice to be one deserving of the name!

Bitterly did mother and brother feel that they should, however unwillingly, have been the cause of Mary's trouble. But she knew she had chosen the best way; she had implored the guidance of the Lord, and sought His counsel about the matter, and so she knew all would be well. Often she said to herself, 'By-and-by I will feel better, my heart will surely not always ache thus. When I am settled as a governess, and must give my attention to other things, it will cease to be so.' And three years she had now been in Mr Willoughby's family, and, save in the one fault of strict discipline, she had fulfilled all her duties.

Yet she had to confess her heart ached still; and whenever she heard the name of Ainsworth, a great sickness came over her from some unexplained cause. She heard Mr Willoughby read aloud the name of Herbert Ainsworth's regiment as one of those ordered to the seat of war, and the colour suddenly left her cheek, and a strange rushing was in her ears; but she fainted not. She said to herself, Herbert was nothing to her—nothing. Most likely he was married by this time, 'only, you know, one can't help feeling anxious about an old friend.' No one had observed her paleness, so no remark was made; none knew her sorrow; her own sore and her own grief, like those of many another, were known only to herself and to the Great King, who, though He inhabiteth eternity, 'knoweth the hearts of the children of men,' and bindeth up the broken spirit.

That night, as Miss Manley knelt in prayer, she realized, as she had never fully done before, the privilege of being not only permitted, but entreated, to cast all her care upon the Lord, for He careth for her.

CHAPTER VIII.

'Whosoever will come after Me, let him deny himself, and take up his cross and follow Me.'—MARK viii. 34.

THE feelings, which had stirred Mr Willoughby's heart on that Sabbath we have written of, were no mere evanescent ones, but the work of the Holy Spirit within him.

He was as a man who woke up suddenly, and found that he had been sleeping when he should have been journeying on important business to a far-off town, and who determined to make up for lost time by extra speed. His whole heart was yielded up to his God, and from that time his one resolve was, 'As for me and my house, we will serve the Lord.'

Family worship had never been neglected, sacred things never despised there; but now they were pervaded with a new spirit—no formal utterances merely, but the glowing expressions of a loving heart. Servants and children alike noticed the change; Ada and Arthur, children-like, did not seek to find out a reason for the change, only they felt they could talk to Mr Willoughby now as they once could not.

'Papa knows so well what one feels,' said Arthur, 'and reads one's very thoughts even when you would rather he did not; and, do you know, he finds it is not always easy to do what is right, just as we feel. To-day, when I had finished the Latin lesson he always gives me, he looked out, and said he should go now for a ride, the day was so beautiful; and he would perhaps call at Mr Marshman's, and make arrangements about the pic-nic we are to have next week. Well, just then, William the butler came in with a whole lot of papers in his hand, and said that these were the estimates for the new cottages papa is building near the large meadow, and Mr Sandford would be obliged by his letting him know as soon as convenient if they pleased him. Papa looked vexed, but said, "Very well, he would see about them," stood a moment undecided, then, taking up the papers in his hand, sat down at his desk. "Aint you going to ride, papa?" I said. "No," he answered, "I cannot now, for these papers will occupy me a long time, and you know I cannot put them off till the evening, as we have friends dining with us, and I must settle about them to-day. I would far rather have taken the ride, Arthur, but 'duty before pleasure;' and you know we are not put into this world to do only those things which please ourselves. The Great King tells us to deny ourselves; and He says in His Word, 'Be not slothful in business, but fervent in spirit, serving the Lord.' So you see the ride must wait, and these accounts be done, and the sooner the better. So, my boy, you must go for the present."

'And, Ada, ever since,' continued Arthur, 'I have been thinking how strange it is that papa also has to do things he does not like, just like us children; but then he does it always to please the Great King. I wish I could do that too, Ada, always; but it is sometimes so hard to do—to have to leave off reading some curious story, or beautiful poem, just because the school-bell rings; or to stop arranging my case of butterflies, because Frances says, "Oh! Arthur, come and see this;" or, do you know, to-day I felt just the same when papa called me to come to my Latin lesson five minutes earlier than usual. These are the sorts of things I feel so wrong about, and at the time I forget to ask the Great King to help me to do right. Ada, do you feel so?'

'Yes,' Ada told him, 'often, often;' and then they began to wonder why people felt it so difficult to do the right thing. 'Oh, if Eve had not taken the apple, then, you know, no one would ever have wished to do wrong.' All unconsciously they were verging to a subject which has puzzled the heads of so-called wise men for ages—the permission of evil. Well for the children, who truly were getting beyond their depth, that the school-bell rung; and, finding it better to obey than reason, they ran off. And it would be well for the so-called wise men, if, leaving fruitless speculations, they listened to the voice of Him who cannot lie, who has promised, that 'what we know not now, we shall know hereafter.'

The terror Mr Willoughby had taken about his boy's health had not altogether subsided. There was an increased brightness in his eye, a more delicate colour in his cheeks, and a marked want of strength. Anxiously did both father and mother watch these symptoms, and at once consulted the doctor who had attended him from his birth. He examined the boy, but said little, except that there was no cause for present alarm; indeed, he thought the child no worse than usual; desired him to be kept as much as possible in the open air, but not allowed to overtire himself; not to overwork him at his lessons; at the same time by no means to let him give them up, as they occupied his mind, which inclined too much to prey on itself; but with care he saw no cause for present anxiety.

Mrs Willoughby seemed relieved by the doctor's opinion; but his father had caught a strong accent on the word 'present,' and a cloud of anxiety rested on his heart. Once such a cloud would have bowed him to the ground in despair; now it led him to the Mercy-seat, to ask for grace to help in time of need, for strength to learn in *all* things to say, 'Thy will, not mine, be done.'

He now kept a greater oversight of the children than he had formerly done, instructing the three in Bible lessons every day, opening up the Scriptures to them. Frances took pleasure in these lessons, because she liked to be taught by her papa; the others, because they learned more to know the will of the Great King.

One day they read of Josiah, the young king of Judah, son of Amon, how he did that which was right in the sight of the Lord, and declined not to the right hand nor to the left. 'Notice, children,' said Mr Willoughby, 'while he was yet young, he began to seek after God, and made all the idols and the carved images be removed, that God might reign alone; and he repaired the house of the Lord, and made the words of the Law, which the Great King had imparted to Moses, and which had long lain neglected, be read aloud to all the people; and he himself, going up to the house of God, and standing before the people, declared, before the Lord, that his desire was to keep His commandments and His statutes with his whole heart, and to do the things which were written in the Book.'

Arthur listened eagerly to his father's words, and, waiting till the others had gone away, begged him to tell him what he could do for God. 'You know, papa, there are no idols here that I can throw down, no church I can repair, no people I can read the Bible to who know it not.'

'No idols here, you say, Arthur? What if I were to tell you there are, and that I have noticed several times there is one you worship and obey?'

'Me, papa, obey an idol! Oh! no, no.'

'Yes, Arthur, the idol you can, by God's help, cast down is—Self. Too often I see you obey its voice rather than that of the Great King. Only on Saturday last, I heard Claude ask you three times over, when you were looking over the large book of prints, to come out and have a game with him; and your answer was, "Presently, when I am tired of this book, but not now."'

'Yes, papa, I remember; Claude was vexed, and said he had promised Frances and Ada to walk with them in a short time, and unless I could come at once we could not have the game; and I said, "Well, it would wait till some other time." But that was a very small thing, papa: surely that was not obeying the commands of Self; that could not be like worshipping an idol.'

'First tell me what is an idol,' said Mr Willoughby.

'Oh! anything that we put in the place of God, and care more for than we do for Him; you told us so the other day.'

'Well, Arthur, how are we to show our love to

God save by doing His commands? What says He in His Word? "Be ye kind one to another, tender-hearted, forgiving one another, even as God for Christ's sake hath forgiven you" (Ephes. iv. 32). Please not yourself; even Christ pleased not Himself. But the idol, Self, tells you only to do those things which are agreeable and pleasant to you, and not to care about the pleasures of others at all. Now, when you refused Claude's simple request, whom did you obey, the Great King or Self? Well, if you would do what is pleasing to the Lord, strive to cast down that idol within your heart, that the Holy Spirit may dwell there alone. In the strength of the Lord Josiah did all things, and it is by His help alone that you can do so also. Self, my boy, is a great stumbling-stone in your way to the palace of the Great King. Ask the Guide who holds your hand, even Jesus, to lift you right over it, so that you fall not.'

Mr Willoughby spoke very earnestly, for he saw that a great fault in Arthur's character was indulging self. Made an object of care and solicitude from infancy, this trait in his character was fostered and increased, and, but for the grace of God, would spread and hinder his heavenward way.

Arthur owned the truth of his father's words; and as he was, not in word only, but in reality, seeking to walk in the narrow way, he became most desirous to conquer self, to be a true follower of Him who came into the world not to be ministered unto, but to minister.

The children of the Great King of whom we write were not perfect; but becoming changed, as it were, from glory to glory, pressing on to the kingdom.

CHAPTER IX.

'Let those refuse to sing
  Who never knew our God;
But servants of the heavenly King
  Should speak their joy abroad.
The hill of Zion yields
  A thousand sacred sweets,
Before we reach the heavenly fields,
  Or walk the golden streets.'

'ISN'T this a glorious morning for our pic-nic, Miss Manley?' were the words which greeted that lady's ears as she entered the school-room one Saturday morning, and found Frances, Ada, Arthur, and Claude preparing already for the long-talked of pic-nic.

They were wild with delight; several friends were to join them—the Mitford girls from Ashton Park, as well as Mr Marshman and his pupils. Papa and mamma, and Miss Manley, were to accompany them; and after a long drive they were to climb up a hill, and have dinner under some fine old trees, from which spot one of the finest views of the neighbouring country was to be had. Claude and Arthur had armed themselves with small hammers and tin cases, to get specimens of stones, and particularly of the bright pink marble which abounds in these parts; and the girls also carried small botanical cases, hoping to collect wild flowers, and perhaps get some new kind of fern for the fernery.

By ten o'clock the whole party had assembled; the carriage and waggonette were at the door; and, after a large amount of bustle and commotion, Mr Willoughby succeeded in getting them all seated and fairly started, all declaring loudly it was a shame not to let dear little Minnie come also; but mamma would by no means consent to such a proposal, telling them Minnie would soon get wearied and wish to go home.

On they drove through shady lanes, past verdant meadows and rich corn-fields, where the reapers were busy at work, pausing only a moment as the party passed by, to gaze at the bright, happy young faces, and, it may be, heave a sigh that their own lot was one of toil; but for all that they wished in their hearts that the young people might have a pleasant day. Presently the road passed along the foot of a beautifully wooded hill, the trees overshadowing the carriages as they passed. A little farther on, and the sea, sparkling under the rays of an August sun, burst on their sight.

Where is the child who exults not at the sight of the sea, wild, free, and boundless, coming from where they know not, leading to lands unknown? Or is it, that in its ever changing, restless waves they feel a response to the ever surging emotions of their own young hearts?

But the road once more strikes inland; the party alight at an old-fashioned farm-house, and, leaving the horses to be put up, proceed to clamber up a neighbouring hill. The elders of the party proceed leisurely, and at first try to keep a sort of order amongst the youngsters; but, finding this impossible, resign the task with a smile, only insisting that the young people wait at the top till they join them.

Promising to do so, they set off, Frances and Ada taking the lead with the girls, and Claude with the boys. They agreed that they would go straight up to the top of the hill, and then set some game a-going; and if going straight up meant darting aside first to one part, then to another, in search of some flower or insect, and running always farther into the wood, because some new beauty struck their eye, they certainly accomplished their plan. But when they did arrive at the top, they were rather surprised to find that the slow walkers, as they termed the older division of the party, had arrived before them, having really kept to the right road.

Mr Marshman taunted them with being sluggards,

and related in a most humorous way the fable of the hare and the tortoise. The story was received with shouts of laughter. They had all heard it often before, but what of that? it does not take much to make one laugh when the heart is gay, and one is at a pic-nic.

An open part of the hill was discovered, the very place for games; and there for some time they were carried on, the boys jumping, wrestling, running races, etc., the girls at quieter plays: croquet was not yet become a prevailing mania; so blind man's buff, puss in the corner, through the needle-eye, and the like, did instead. Frances, had the Miss Roscoes been there, might have pronounced those games decidedly childish and slow, and rather have preferred to join the sports of the boys, as more suitable to the tastes of those young ladies who are desirous of approaching as nearly as possible to the other sex. But away from the influence of her foolish cousins, Frances was becoming more natural, and thoroughly enjoyed herself.

The games finished, the great sport was to assist in laying out the dinner. A beautiful spot was chosen, shaded partly by the trees, and yet open enough to let the eye wander over an extensive view of hill and dale, and the more distant sea. Close by murmured a little brook, clear as crystal, here dashing over its rocky bed, hasting away to the ocean. The dinner disappeared in some marvellous way amidst a perfect flow of talk and laughter, drowning the song of the larks that soared over-head, and startling the wood-pigeons from their gentle cooing.

Then began a vigorous search for wild flowers, ferns, stones, and the pink marble, some of which was to be found in the neighbourhood. Some of the children, accompanied by Mr Willoughby, followed the course of the little river a good way. In some parts it was very beautiful, cutting out a bed for itself through rocks overshadowed by trees, through the varied green of which quivered the rays of the sun, resting not till they touched the water and played on its ripples. Beautiful species of ferns grew on the banks, and many delicately tinted wild flowers raised their slender forms there, seeming as if they also loved the wild spot; and the dog-roses threw clusters of their bright-coloured berries over the stream, as if to repay it for the refreshing moisture with which it supplied their roots.

Ada was especially charmed with the beauties of the place. All was new to her, and she fancied everything in this wooded hill looked fair and fresh, as it must have done the very morning of the creation, while it still wore the impress of the Creator's hand. She could have loitered there for ever, but a proposal was made to leave the rivulet and go elsewhere; but before they went, Claude struck up (and was soon joined by the voices of the others) the song of the Brook :—

> 'I come from haunts of coot and hern,
>   I make a sudden sally;
> And sparkle out among the fern,
>   To bicker down a valley.
> By thirty hills I hurry down,
>   Or slip between the ridges;
> By twenty thorps, a little town,
>   And half a hundred bridges.'

The song described so exactly the little brook before them, that some of the youngsters thought Claude had improvised it for the occasion, and applauded accordingly. The woods echoed back the chorus, then let it softly die away; and, leaving the little brook to its accustomed solitude, the party started off in another direction.

Of all the merry party that day, none were more so than Claude, Ada, and Arthur; distinguished only by a greater willingness to yield up their own wishes to the rest, by a greater eagerness not to please themselves so much as others. Mr Marshman noticed Ada's behaviour all that day closely; he wished to judge for himself if Claude's account of his sister was a true one, and if so, if he could find it out by her conduct. For Claude had told him, that whatever he was himself, he was quite sure Ada was a child of the Great King.

Now Mr Marshman remembered that there are certain tests revealed in the will of the King, whereby His children may be known: these are love, joy, peace, long-suffering, gentleness, goodness, meekness, temperance, faith; and he looked to see some marks of these in Ada. He was not long in doubt: in her gentle courtesy, her willingness to help the others, and her complete unselfishness, he read her right to the title her brother had given her.

One little incident confirmed his opinion. With great delight Ada had shown him a beautiful plant of the *Adiantum capillus veneris* fern. 'I just require it,' she said, 'to make up my collection. Is not it a beauty?'

Just then, Bertha Mitford came running up. 'Oh, Ada, what a lucky girl you are, to have got a plant of that! I would give anything to get one, for Charlotte and I have looked for it for weeks, and have not got one.'

A moment Ada stood irresolute, a bright flush mantling her cheek. Words of the Great King were before her eyes. 'Be ye kind one to another.' The next, she was begging Bertha to accept the fern; begging her in such a pleasant way, that the girl did not see the giving it up had cost her a struggle, and she took it with many thanks.

Mr Marshman had watched the scene, and observed Ada's mental struggle. He put his hand kindly on her shoulder, saying, 'A new commandment,' said the Son of the King ere He left the earth, 'I give unto you; that ye love one another, as I have loved you. By this shall all men know that ye are My disciples, if ye have love one to another.'

Ada looked up smilingly at the words. 'Oh, but it was such a little thing to do, and she did so wish it.' Then she bounded off with a step light as a young fawn, the brightest of the bright young band.

Who dare say that religion is a gloomy thing; that the servants of Satan, who groan under his iron yoke here, and have in prospect nought but endless misery hereafter, are the happy ones, whilst the redeemed children of the King of kings, to whom belong all the cheering promises and the certainty of never-ending bliss, are to be condoled with as sad and melancholy creatures? Ay, who suggests such an idea, save he who was a liar from the beginning, even the father of lies? Listen not to him; answer him in the only language he fears, the language of the Great King; tell him it is false: 'The children of Zion are joyful in their King;' on their banners, emblazoned in letters of gold, stand the words, 'Rejoicing in the Lord.' Through trials and sorrows, through life, and even in the dark shadow of death, they, and they only, can say, 'We joy in God through the Lord Jesus Christ, through whom we have now received the atonement;' and the dark valley passed, the river crossed, the city of everlasting day entered, what hear we there? The voice of a great multitude of redeemed ones, who sing, Alleluia: the Lord God omnipotent reigneth.' Let us be glad and rejoice, and give honour to Him.

Whilst the party were thus roaming about, Arthur, tired with the day's unwonted fatigues, was lying quietly by his father's side; now showing him the different stones and beautiful pieces of marble he had collected, now tranquilly enjoying the lovely view before him, his eye resting now on the darkly wooded hills, now on the bright blue sea, glimpses of which were caught here and there through the openings of the trees; and the white sails of the ships, as they glided past, glimmered in the bright sunshine. Close by babbled the little stream, a gentle breeze murmured amongst the leafy trees, and swept gently over the long grass. It was as if nature were singing a more than usually sweet hymn of praise. The whish, whish of the trees; the ripple, ripple of the brook; the soft cooing of the doves; and the chirp, chirp of many of the feathered tribe,—all mingled and produced a dreary, slumberous feeling.

Father and son sat long in silence. At last Mr Willoughby broke it, repeating distinctly words which the scene had suggested to him: 'O Lord my God, Thou art very great: who coverest Thyself with light as with a garment; who stretchest out the heavens like a curtain. He sendeth the springs into the valleys, which run among the hills. They give drink to every beast in the forest; by them the fowls of heaven have their habitation, which sing amongst the branches.'

'Oh, papa, how true all that is!' said Arthur; 'do you know I have just been thinking, although that brook is such a little one, how useful it is. Look how green everything is that grows near it, how fresh the trees and flowers are, how the little birds love it, and how merry it seems. That, I suppose, is because it is never idle; and yet all the time it is flowing on, on to its eternity, the ocean. I wish I could be like it, always working usefully, always happy, yet never forgetting the end. Papa, say something to me, something of Milton's. I never weary of hearing his poems.'

He listened with delight as his father repeated long passages from 'Paradise Lost.' Nature around them seemed fair as that of Paradise, and both felt as if the poet merely gave expression to their own inner thoughts.

> 'These are Thy glorious works, Parent of good,
> Almighty; this Thy universal frame,
> How wondrous fair! Thyself how wondrous then!'

They were interrupted by Claude, who, buoyant with health and spirits, came dashing down upon them. 'Poetizing, Arthur, I declare; and uncle too!

Come, that is too bad, when we are all waiting for you to join in a game. Come along, and leave Milton for some other time.'

Arthur rose quickly, but Mr Willoughby stopped him. 'No, Claude, Arthur has had more than enough of fatigue to-day, and is better to rest a while; so go off, and leave us in peace to our poetizing, as you call it.'

Claude's eye rested on Arthur, and his flushed cheek and wearied appearance showed him at a glance that his uncle was right; and in his impetuous, kind-hearted fashion, he volunteered to stay with him and cheer him a bit; 'only, Arthur, I am not going to quote Milton to you, for, to tell you the truth, I don't care much about him. I like poems about battles. To be sure there are battles in "Paradise Lost" too, but not the kind I care about. Do you know Macaulay's "Lays?" they are splendid. Here goes for his Henry of Navarre!' And, standing up, he declaimed it with great spirit, ending with the declaration, 'That's what I call something of a poem; that is the kind of soldier I mean to be.' Then, without waiting for further remarks, he ran off, suddenly remembering he had promised the others to come back immediately.

Mr Willoughby and Arthur looked after him, laughing at his abrupt departure. 'Papa,' said Arthur, 'is not he a splendid fellow? and won't he make a famous soldier?'

'Yes, he certainly is a fine boy, and has a true soldier spirit. I wish his father could have seen him now. I am glad you and your cousins get on so well, Arthur ; you love them both, don't you ?'

'Yes, papa, that I do. Ada is so good and kind, and pretty too ; and Claude—you don't know how I admire him. I believe he'll be a hero some day. I never read of Leonidas, Bonaparte, or the Duke of Wellington, without thinking Claude will be like some of these.'

Mr Willoughby smiled at the different sorts of men Arthur had fixed upon for Claude to resemble, but was pleased to hear his boy speak so fondly of his cousin.

The day was indeed a happy one to all parties, one of those days to be long remembered with pleasure, and looked back upon when the cares and trials of life are pressing on the hearts, so young and light now ; and, perchance, with the very remembrance thereof, would spring up softer feelings and holier thoughts, redolent of leafy trees, silvery streams, flowers, birds, summer sunshine, and often also of loved ones, who since that day have fallen asleep in Jesus.

Just as the party were leaving the hill preparatory to getting into the carriages on their way home, Mr Marshman put into Ada's hand a plant of the fern she had given to Bertha Mitford. 'I was determined to find one,' he said jokingly, 'in order that you might not think yourself the only clever searcher of the party. And see here it is for you; you can call it the Marshman hair fern, if you like, in remembrance of me. Long ago a decoction used to be made from its juice, called capillaire, which, it was said, made ladies' hair beautiful.'

Ada's look thanked him more than her words, and she drove home, holding her treasure with no small delight.

The sun was far down in the west when the picnic party arrived at Willoughby House, all pleased and happy, but willing, ere the night was far advanced, to seek their couches, and go over the pleasures of the day in dreams.

Long may they continue to find happiness in such simple joys, long retain the child-like spirit which seeks and finds amidst the scenes of nature the purest pleasure!

CHAPTER X.

'He that dwelleth in the secret place of the Most High, shall abide under the shadow of the Almighty.'—Ps. xci. 1.

WHILST the Percy children were passing their time thus quietly in their pleasant Devonshire home, far other were the scenes in which their father mingled.

The English and French armies were still awaiting at Varna the command to set out for the Crimea, and commence the attack on the strongly fortified town of Sebastopol. Somewhat impatiently they waited; all longed for action, many chafed under the delay; but as long as possible the order was kept back. Whilst waiting this, cholera attacked first the French army, afterwards the English: fearful was the loss of life. Rumours, perhaps exaggerated, reached our country, and penetrated to the homes of Devon, where many a house, like other counties in the kingdom, possessed dear ones in that army.

A letter from Colonel Percy to his children told the real facts of the case, which, although less fearful than common report, were still bad enough. An extract from his letter we give :—

'DEAREST CHILDREN,—In spite of many pressing duties, I seize one quiet moment to write to you. Ere this time, you will have heard what devastation cholera is making both in our army and that of the French. The real state of things is bad enough, but newspaper reports will make them worse; so I caution you not to believe all you hear. Well do I know how anxious you will be to hear of my safety; and, thank God, I am in as good health as I have ever been in my life, though cast down, it is true, by the death and illness of many loved comrades, and by the sufferings around.

'Solemn feeling, that in the very midst of life we are in death! But yet, dear ones, I am able to say of the Great King, "He is my refuge, and my fortress; my God, in Him will I trust." Under the cover of His wings I am not afraid for the pestilence that walketh in darkness, nor for the destruction that wasteth at noonday. To live amid such scenes, and have no abiding trust in God, no assurance of interest in Christ, were sad indeed.

'Dear children, if you could hear, as I do, from many lips the mournful, wailing regrets that Christ was not sought after in health, you would feel in truth the great importance of not putting off coming to

Jesus till death comes. I have been by many death-beds, able, I trust, to help and comfort some.

'One dear friend, by whose bed I had sat for many days, looking for his death (and longing to hear one word from his lips to tell of his hope in Christ, of which I could know nothing), this morning, to the amazement of all, has rallied, and the doctor thinks he is in a fair way of recovery. The first words he said were, "Pray, pray; death has been very near me, and I was not prepared; I have never thought of my God in the days of health, as I should. If He spares me, with His help my life shall be a different one. Say that verse again: 'If any man sin, we have an advocate (I finished it) with the Father, Jesus Christ the righteous; and He is the propitiation for our sins.'" Whilst repeating the words, he fell asleep, and awoke much better. He is a young officer of the name of Ainsworth, with whom I have only lately become acquainted; but I knew his father some years ago, when our regiment was quartered in Yorkshire, in which county he had a property.

'In Claude's last letter he asks me how I can endure to stop here doing nothing while all that fighting is going on, and exalts the brave conduct of the young Englishmen who went to the immediate help of the Turks; but Claude, my boy, you forget that a soldier is fully doing his duty when he is obeying the orders of his leader, whosoever he may be. He must learn to wait as well as fight, and it can never be a soldier's part to question whether his leader is giving right orders or not. When he gives the word, all are ready, nay, longing to go; but, till then, our duty is to wait in patience. If every soldier were to do only that which was right in his own eyes, where were discipline, and what would our army be worth? And if this be so in earthly things, how much more so in heavenly? Our duty must always be to obey, not our own inclinations, but the orders of the Captain of our salvation: where He points the way, to follow; where He forbids us to go, to go not. An earthly leader may err, the Great King can never. The young Englishmen you write of are noble fellows; and as they were then under no command, they were fully justified in acting the bold part they did.

'But do not be afraid, Claude; we are not going to leave all the honour to them. We put full trust in our commander, and know that, when the right time comes, he will not hang back. Already reports are going, that orders from England have arrived, telling us to set off. If so, none will rejoice more than your affectionate father, who commends you both, now and always, to the loving protection of your Father in heaven, who is present everywhere.'

Ada's voice trembled as she read the letter, and

her heart failed her. She saw nothing but danger on all hands for her father. Even if he escaped cholera, still there was the danger of the battle-fields before him. The danger he was in had never come so forcibly before her, and Claude was not beside her to laugh away her fears. She had read the letter aloud to her uncle and aunt alone; when she had finished it, Mrs Willoughby noticed the deadly paleness of her face, and strove to comfort her, telling her she should be very thankful that her papa was so well, and wrote in such good spirits.

Yes, Ada acknowledged she should be so; 'only you know,' said she, 'that letter is written days ago, and the cholera was still raging, and papa might have got it now, or even be dead.' And saying that, she laid down her head, and burst into tears. No need to repress them now, she thought; she had no papa near, to be distressed at the sight.

Mrs Willoughby looked and felt troubled; but her uncle soothed Ada, quietly drawing her to his arms, and, reminding her she was distressing herself unnecessarily, began to talk to her about the letter, and by degrees got her to answer him, and to interest herself about her father's new friend, Mr Ainsworth, till, in thinking of others, she forgot her own grief. But once more there came a deep sob, and a heartfelt exclamation, 'Oh, if I only knew papa was safe!'

Ada,' whispered her uncle, 'can you not trust him to the keeping of the Great King?'

She said nothing, but left the room to call Frances and Arthur to their Bible-reading.

Mr Willoughby spoke chiefly that day on the verse, 'He shall fear no evil tidings whose heart is fixed, trusting in the Lord.'

'The servants of the Great King,' he said, 'have no right to be always looking forward to evil, seeing all the mercies we are every day receiving from Him should rather lead us to expect blessing than evil. And, besides, if we really trust in Him, we know that whatever happens to us, painful though it seem, will yet in the end prove good to us, and not evil.'

He then spoke of Christ's command, 'Take no thought for the morrow: sufficient unto the day is the evil thereof.' 'If grief is coming on us, time enough to bear it when it comes; no need to go half-way to meet it.' As he spoke, his eye rested on his boy, and he felt he himself sorely needed to learn the very lesson he was trying to teach others.

Have not we all a like need? how many an anxious restless night, how many a bitter tear and an aching heart, would be spared us, if we would cease to look forward to evils which, perhaps, never really come at all, and, looking only to the present, learn the full truth of the promise, 'that as our day is, so shall our strength be.'

When school hours were over, Miss Manley asked Ada about her letter. Eagerly the child related some particulars of it, dwelling on the account given of Captain Ainsworth. So engrossed was she with the story, that she failed to observe Miss Manley's agitation at the mention of the name and the illness. But Arthur, who was sitting beside them, and chanced to be looking at Miss Manley, saw a strange expression come over her face, and, starting forward, asked if she were ill, and if he could get anything for her. By a strong mental effort she roused herself, and thanking Arthur, said she felt sick and faint, and would go and lie down awhile.

For some minutes after she reached her room, she sat like one in a dream; only one thought in her mind, one sight before her eyes: Herbert Ainsworth ill and dying, far from home. If she had ever deceived herself into the belief that she no longer loved him, she was undeceived now. Oh! to see him once more, to hear him speak, to have one word of kindness from him! 'I could lay down my life to save him; for oh, how I love him!' was the confession coming from her in that moment.

But not long could she indulge her grief; she had duties to perform, and in silence she must bear her own burden. She had no right that the world would acknowledge that she should grieve thus for one who had clearly shown he no longer valued her love.

Only one thing she might do; she could pray for him, pray that if it were the will of God he might yet be spared, and prove a true follower of Him who had made atonement for him.

Blessed indeed are the children of the Great King in this, their inestimable privilege of prayer. Through Christ Jesus, they are permitted to enter into the very presence-chamber of the King, and there, with full confidence in His sympathizing love, to tell Him every difficulty, every little sorrow, and every care, and seek His guidance. Griefs that can be told to no earthly friends, can be communicated to Him who lends an ever-patient ear, and upbraideth not. Alas! how seldom even His own children avail themselves as they might of their glorious privilege! Often they scarcely value it till the hour of sore suffering, when man's compassion fails to relieve, and leads them to seek that of Him, who alone is able to comfort those that mourn, and give them beauty for ashes, the oil of joy for mourning, the garment of praise for the spirit of heaviness.

Few remarks were made on Miss Manley's sudden indisposition. 'What has become of Miss Manley?' said Frances, as she came into the school-room soon after she had left. Ada told her she had felt faint, and gone to lie down a little.

'Then,' said she, 'perhaps I had better go and see how she is.'

'I would not, if I were you,' said Arthur. 'I think she wanted to be left quite alone.'

'Oh, well,' Frances said, 'if that is what she wishes, I will not go near her; only mamma will say it was unkind.'

Ada would at once have followed Miss Manley and seen her lie comfortably down; but Arthur had held her back, and said that he was quite sure she would rather be alone. 'Ada,' said he, 'you can't think what a strange look came over her face just as you read out Captain Ainsworth's name. I should not wonder if he is an old friend, and she turned faint when she heard how ill he was.'

But Ada did not think that was at all likely, because, had it been the case, she would have told them so, and it would have quite accounted for her sudden illness. 'Oh, no, it was just as she had said, a slight faintness,' and so the subject passed; and when, shortly after, Miss Manley came in, looking pale and grave it is true, but saying she was better now, Ada was confirmed in her own opinion. But Arthur, although he spoke no more of it, could not help thinking that Miss Manley knew Captain Ainsworth, and was very sorry he was ill.

CHAPTER XI.

'Yes, man for man perchance may brave
The horrors of the yawning grave.
And friend for friend, or child for sire,
Undaunted and unmoved expire,
From love, or piety, or pride.
But who can die as Jesus died?'

NOT far from Willoughby House lay the pretty little village of Ashton. The houses which constituted it were not numerous, and were inhabited entirely by the working classes, most of whom were agricultural labourers. At the farther end of the village, at the foot of a wooded declivity, was the parsonage, and at a short distance from it the village church.

The clergyman was a young man, who had only been a few months in the parish, but who had already won all hearts by his frank, open manners, unwearied kindness, and attention to his duties. Keen critics might have said that his sermons were far from clever, more remarkable for simplicity than depth; and possibly it was so. But they were faithful expositions of the will of God concerning man, and clear declarations of the Gospel of Christ, of the only way of salvation. No thirsting soul went to that church, longing to know what to do to be saved, and came away in doubt as to the way. 'Believe in the Lord Jesus Christ, and ye shall be saved;' 'Come to Him, and ye have His own promise,—He that cometh to Me, I will in no wise cast out,' was the substance of the message which they received as suited to their wants. They felt as if the minister had read their very hearts.

Many might have desired the advantages of a more learned ministry, but his simple-minded hearers were well pleased; and, at all events, the food with which they were fed, if not strongly savoured with earthly learning, was composed of the purest Gospel nourishment; and many lived to bless the day when they heard the Gospel message so faithfully and simply delivered in the parish church.

Nor were his sermons confined to the pulpit, but they were continued in his life during the week. His delight was in his Master's work; and the peace and joy which dwelt in his heart showed itself in his walk and conversation, and proclaimed, as loudly as words could do, that the Master he served was a good one, His yoke an easy one, and His burden light. Mr Willoughby was much attracted by the young minister; and together they engaged in many a labour of love,

Mr Hole often obtaining much assistance in any difficulty from Mr Willoughby's clear judgment.

The young clergyman became a frequent visitor at Willoughby House, and was a great favourite with the young members of it; Arthur especially loving to hear him talk, because, as he told Ada, his heart was so full of love to the Son of the Great King.

'He could not help speaking of Him,' said he. 'And, do you know, when I said to him the other day that I did so like everything that was beautiful, he asked me if I remembered that all these things were the gifts of the Lord, and that I must never forget that His most precious gift to the children of men is His only Son, who is altogether lovely. Then he made me notice the names of beauty which are given to Jesus: 'The Rose of Sharon,' 'The Lily of the Valley,' 'The Apple Tree of the Wood,' with its beautiful hanging fruit, 'The Plant of Renown,' 'The Bright and Morning Star;' and, Ada, isn't it very pleasant to think that the Guide who is leading us all the way to the palace of the Great King, is so beautiful?'

Ada said she liked to think of that very well, but what she liked best of all, was to know that Jesus held her in His firm grasp, and would not let her go, because she was so little able to do right in her own strength; that, but for Him, she would, she knew, turn aside, and never, never reach the palace at all.

'Ada,' said Mr Hole one day, 'have you never a

spare hour you could give to read a little to a poor blind woman in the village? She is alone almost all day, and, poor body, is lonely enough, not even being accustomed to it, like many blind people, for she has only turned so lately.'

'Oh yes, I could,' was the eager reply; 'on Wednesday we have always a half-holiday, and are allowed to do what we like; and then on Saturdays I could, and would like it so much. Stay a moment; of course I must ask aunt's leave first.'

Mrs Willoughby had no objections to the plan. She knew well about old Mrs Barnes, and if Ada liked, certainly she might, and she dared say Frances would also go sometimes; but Frances cut her part of the matter very short, by declaring that Ada might do as she liked, but she had no desire to become a reader to old women, to please Mr Hole or any other person.

'Oh, Frances!' exclaimed Ada, 'I don't wish to do it merely to please Mr Hole, but I would like to help to cheer a poor blind woman. Think how very, very dull she must be, not able to see anything; and, besides, I will like to do it to please'— She stopped short, for she saw Mr Hole had moved across the room, and must have overheard the conversation.

He stepped forward to her, and said he was glad she had got her aunt's permission; as the next day was Wednesday, perhaps, if her uncle, who was coming to the parsonage at all events in the afternoon, would bring her with him, he would like to go with her himself and introduce her to Mrs Barnes. 'She is a true servant of the Lord's, I believe,' said he; 'and in helping His servants we are helping Him. Even now from heaven the Great King is saying to His children, "Inasmuch as ye do it unto one of the least of these My brethren, ye do it unto Me."'

Ada soon glided away to talk to her uncle, leaving Mr Hole and Frances alone. He had overheard Frances's speech, and felt it a duty to give her a word of reproof; but how to do so wisely perplexed him, not so much from a fear of offending her, as of repelling, and thus marring, his power of perhaps influencing her for good, as her father had once or twice urged him to do.

Frances, fearing he might have heard her speech, felt somewhat constrained when left alone with him; but Mr Hole put her at ease by asking her some simple questions. Then, changing the conversation, he asked her if there had been any letters lately from her uncle, Colonel Percy.

'Yes,' Frances answered; 'and he writes that a report was going that orders from England had arrived, desiring them to set out for the Crimea. Of course uncle was very anxious to be off; and, Mr Hole, don't you admire those young officers, Nasmyth,

Butler, and Ballard, and the other four, who have helped the Turks so bravely? But for them, uncle wrote some time ago, Silistria must have fallen; and they say the Turks love them so, they would do anything for them. And well they may: poor Captain Butler received his death-wound fighting to save their lives. I am sure it is no wonder they think highly of them.'

'No, indeed, Miss Willoughby, they have a good claim on their affection, and for their sakes should be glad, nay anxious, to help any Englishman, should an opportunity be given to him; shouldn't you think so?'

'Oh, certainly,' replied Frances, 'it would be the best manner of showing their gratitude to those, one of whom, at least, died to save them. But, Mr Hole, you look grave; was Captain Butler a friend or relation of yours?'

'No, oh no,' said Mr Hole; 'but my thoughts turned to a Friend who laid down His own life to save mine, and I was thinking that the best way I could show my grateful remembrance of what He had done for me was by helping His friends.'

'Laid down his life for you, Mr Hole; how?' exclaimed Frances.

'And for you also, Miss Willoughby. What friend has done for us what the Lord Jesus has done? so loved us as to die for us? How have you shown your gratitude to Him, in return for all He has done? He asks you to give Him your heart. Ask yourself if you have done so. Were He now on earth, would you not like to do all you could to help and comfort Him? and when He tells you that if you do so to His people, He will regard it as done to Himself, will you turn a deaf ear to His words?'

Frances was touched by the earnestness of Mr Hole's words, and said frankly, 'I see you heard what I said to Ada about the poor woman; but I did not think of it in that way, only I would not care about reading to those kind of people; and—and'—

She stopped, for she was going to quote one of Miss Roscoe's speeches, to the effect that she did not wish to be one of your very good people, who are righteous over-much. She had thought this speech a very clever one when Emily Roscoe had made it; but even her bold spirit quailed under Mr Hole's earnest eye, and so she left the sentence unfinished.

Mr Hole regarded her steadily. 'All the children of the Great King,' he said, 'love to do His will. They that are not His children, are the children of the prince of the powers of darkness. Remember it is to those on His left hand that, at the day of judgment, the Great Judge shall say, "Inasmuch as ye did it not unto one of the least of these My brethren, ye did it not unto Me." If you would not desire to be one of those on the left hand, then seek now, Miss Willoughby, pardon through the blood of Jesus ; and remember the Great King hath promised, that they who seek Him early *shall* find Him.'

Frances gave no response to his words, and Mr Hole rose and joined the rest of the party, but not without a secret prayer, that the words spoken might take effect in the girl's heart. Had he heard her an hour afterwards, teasing Ada about turning a Scripture-reader, and asking her what payment she expected for her trouble, he would have judged that the words spoken had been spoken in vain ; but the seed sown does not at once spring up, and appear above ground. Sometimes it may lie long deep down in the earth ; and whilst men are saying, 'It will never spring up at all,' the Lord of the harvest can send down a shower of refreshing rain upon the very spot, and the little seed will suddenly begin to live, and piercing through the ground set up a small green blade, very small, it may be, at first, but from which in due season will come the ear, and then the full corn in the ear.

CHAPTER XII.

'Ah, Lord God! behold, I cannot speak; for I am a child. But the Lord said, Say not, I am a child: for thou shalt go to all that I shall send thee, and whatsoever I command thee thou shalt speak.'—JER. i. 6, 7.

THERE was no prettier house in the little village than the one in which Widow Barnes lived, built of the granite stone found in the neighbourhood; and, perfectly covered with roses, honeysuckle, and the beautiful scarlet clianthus, it united comfort with beauty.

The little garden, always nicely kept, was well stocked with vegetables and bright flowers of all sorts. A couple of bee-hives might be seen in a corner, whilst, overshadowing the little cottage, were some large apple and pear trees. A small wicket gate led from the village road into the garden; and when Ada, accompanied by Mr Hole, entered it on the Wednesday afternoon we have spoken of, she thought she had never seen a pleasanter spot, and pitied from her heart the poor woman who sat at the door knitting, and yet saw not the beautiful flowers, nor the bright sunshine which was falling on trees and flowers, and colouring the thickly-hanging fruit.

Kindly Mr Hole greeted the blind woman, and told her he had brought a young friend of his to see her, whom he would leave with her a little, while he went elsewhere. At first, Ada felt shy and constrained; but by degrees the old woman's kind talk set her at ease, and she talked away as to an old friend.

'Yet it's dull enough, Miss, sitting here all the day seeing nothing,' said the poor woman; 'and many's the time I weary sorely. The humming of the bees, the chirping of the birdies, and the wind amongst the trees—they're sort of company, you see; and then I can knit a stocking, and I'm better than many a poor blind body, for I can see faces with the eyes of my mind so clear, that times I start up, and can't believe but I see them really. I've two sons living, dear, and a daughter and two sons in the grave. Susan and one of my boys lie yonder in the churchyard, beside their father; but the best and blithest of all, Willie, my sailor boy, lies in a watery grave. I can strew the graves of the others with flowers, but 'tis only tears I can shed for him. Oh! but he was good, and his old mother loved him as the apple of her eye.' And as she spoke, large tears were falling from the blind eyes.

Ada's heart was full of compassion; no set words

of comfort came from her lips, just the simple overflowing of her young trusting soul. 'Oh, Mrs Barnes, don't cry so; if he loved Jesus, he is safe in the golden city, in the palace of the Great King. It must be so pleasant to be there! Only think of the clear river of the waters of life, that always flows there, and of the tree of life with its beautiful leaves, and all manner of fruits; and then, you know, he sees the Lamb of God face to face.'

As she spoke she slipped her hand into the blind mother's. Mrs Barnes spoke not for a while, but the tears ceased to fall, and she pressed the soft young hand in hers, and a quiet thoughtful expression crossed her face.

At last she spoke; it seemed more to herself than to Ada: 'The golden city, the palace of the Great King! Yes, it's there he is. Poor foolish mother that I am, to cry for him, and he there; and even were he here, I could not see him, only I could hear his voice, and it was such a pleasant one; and no doubt I could throw my arms round him and kiss him. Still he must be happier there, in the golden city. Please the Lord, I'll see him there, in the palace of the Great King.'

Ada started, as a child's voice close beside them said, 'Where's that palace, grandmother? Is it a very grand one, like what our Queen lives in; so grand, they say, with ever so many windows in it, and rooms upon rooms? Oh! they do say it's a sight to see.'

'Ay, Willie' ('he is a Willie too,' she said to Ada), 'the palace of the Great King is far grander even than that, and you may live in it if you will. It is up there, Willie, beyond the clouds; it is heaven. Miss here will perhaps tell you about it.'

But as Willie caught sight of Ada's face, he hung his head, and turned bashful.

'Shall I tell you what like it is?' Ada asked. The boy's only answer was an eager look. 'The palace is of pure gold, like clear glass; its walls are of all sorts of beautiful stones, its gates are white and shining, its streets are of gold, and a pure bright river runs there always.'

The boy's eyes were riveted now. 'I'd like to see it,' he said. 'How can I? do tell me.'

'You must ask Jesus to take you there,' said Ada. 'He is the Son of the Great King, and died on the cross for our sins, that all who wish to be His children and do His will may have admittance to the palace. You must ask Him to make you His, Willie, and learn His will. Can you read?'

The boy said no, and ran off.

His grandmother feared it was her fault; 'for all he was seven years old, he only just knew his letters,' she said. 'You see his mother died when he was but a baby; and his father, who is my oldest son, and lives with me, has just petted the bit boy, and never cared to have him learn. And then, since I have got blind these six months past, there was no one near the whole day when his father is out at work; so he said Willie should not go to school for another year, but stop and tend on me. But the boy's keen to learn, and I only wish his father would not think on me, and just let him go with the rest of the village children to school. He is a thoughtful child, and kind to his old grandmother. Well, it may be I'll need no tendance ere long; for the Great King may send for me. Thank you, dear, for speaking about Him; you've done an old body good.'

Just then Mr Hole came in at the wicket, and told Ada she must come now. She shook hands with Mrs Barnes, and promised to come again, then ran out to the road.

Mr Hole lingered a moment: 'Did she cheer you, Mrs Barnes?' he asked.

'That she did, sir, more than she thinks; her simple words went straight to my heart; it is the Lord Himself who is leading her, I think.'

'Well, Ada, how did the reading come on?' Mr Hole said.

Blushing scarlet, Ada owned, with a feeling of shame, 'Oh! I did not read; indeed, Mr Hole, I never thought of it; we only talked. She told me a great deal about her dead son, and I just listened;

and we spoke of the palace of the King, and she seemed pleased. But that was all; it was so little I did. I know, of course, I should have read to her; I knew that was what you asked me to do; perhaps I will manage better another day. Was I very wrong, Mr Hole?'

He smiled at the bright, earnest face raised to his. 'No, no, Ada, I wish to impose no formal rule on you; you must use your own judgment, young as you are. A word of the Great King, spoken in love, often does more good than a whole chapter read as a duty. I hope you have done good, not harm, to-day.'

He parted from her, having seen her, as he had promised Mr Willoughby, safe into the Willoughby grounds. As he watched her a moment, a question, asked eighteen hundred years ago, rose to his lips, 'Who is the greatest in the kingdom of heaven?' He remembered how the Lord Jesus answered the question by calling a little child and setting him in the midst of the questioners; and he rejoiced to think that Jesus was now, as then, a lover of the children, and still warns the worldly and profane, that it were better they were drowned in the depths of the sea than offend one of His little ones.

When Ada reached home, she had to stand a good deal of bantering from Frances, and questioning from Arthur. She had often difficulty in keeping her naturally hot temper in control when Frances bantered her thus; but somehow it did not seem so difficult to-day, for the thought of the patient spirit of the blind woman made it easier. Arthur's questions were answered with pleasure; and when they were alone, she told him about little Willie, and of his wish to learn to read; adding, 'Does not it seem a pity he cannot go to school? and yet it would not be right for Mrs Barnes to be left all alone either.'

'Oh, no! it would not,' said Arthur; 'but, Ada, do you think I could teach him? I would so gladly do it; you know I could go when you go to see the grandmother.'

Ada was delighted with the plan. 'Of course you could, Arthur; you are so clever, you could do anything; and the old woman will be so pleased. I am so glad you have thought of it; only, Arthur, are you sure that'— But something stopped Ada, and she left her sentence unfinished.

'Only what, Ada?' But she turned the subject, and presently Arthur, full of his plan, went to ask his papa's leave to carry it into execution. Eagerly he told his story. Mr Willoughby listened attentively, although he marked with a feeling of pain the delicate flush which mantled the boy's face as he spoke.

'Certainly, Arthur,' said he, 'you have my leave; but remember, if you undertake it, you must carry it out. You had better take the matter into consideration.

You must not forget that your plan will entail your giving up at least two hours of your half-holidays, and so there will be the less time for your favourite books and pursuits. I don't say all this, Arthur, to discourage you; but I think it best you should not begin a thing rashly, and then weary of it, and perhaps complain that you never thought it would interfere with your usual pleasures.'

'No, papa,' said Arthur, 'I will not do that, I have thought of these things; and I know that Ada, too, fears I shall weary of my plan. She did not say it, but I think she was going to do so, and stopped in case I should not like it; but if you will allow me to begin, I think I will not draw back now, because (and he raised his full, soft eyes to his father's) I will ask the Great King to help me, and I know He will.'

'Well, Arthur, then you have my full leave, and best wishes for your success. You will need to exercise patience and forbearance; but, with the blessing of the King, I doubt not you will get on well.'

And so it was, that on Wednesday and Saturday afternoons Ada and Arthur might be seen wending their way through the lanes, bright with autumnal flowers, and crossing stubble fields, as they went to Widow Barnes' cottage, each to pursue their several labours of love. The reading lessons got on capitally, Willie proving a most apt scholar, and conceiving an extraordinary affection for his young teacher;

whilst the blind woman listened with heartfelt attention to the words read by Ada from the book of life, or to those spoken about the things which concern the King.

Times there were when these visits interfered with some holiday pleasure, and a struggle would arise in their hearts, as the great tempter whispered to 'give up Widow Barnes for to-day, just for once.' But it soon passed; the Guide who sustained them taught them how to resist the evil one, till he fled afar off. And so they went on in the path of duty, finding their pleasure in it; and from His throne on high the Son of the Great King looked down on the loving, happy children, and blessed them in their work.

How true it is, that even in this world, whosoever shall give even a cup of cold water to any of Christ's people, because they belong to Him, shall in nowise lose his reward!

CHAPTER XIII.

'The ornament of a meek and quiet spirit, which is in the sight of God of great price.'—1 PET. iii. 4.

'PAPA, did you hear what Charlie Whitmore was telling me about Claude yesterday?' said Frances one morning at breakfast. 'It is the best story I've heard for long. You know Mr Marshman's boys go on Wednesday afternoons to play cricket with the boys at the academy at Portness. Well, it seems that for some time they have been dreadfully jealous of Claude, because he is the best player amongst them, and they have tormented him in all sorts of ways, and called him names, all to make him get up a fight; but Claude was determined not to do so, though Charlie says he knows it was hard work to keep his temper sometimes. But the last day, four or five of the biggest of the Portness boys determined to make him fight, sure they could beat him. Some quarrel about the game took place; so they seized their opportunity, putting the blame of it on Claude.

'"He had nothing to do with it," he protested. "Yes, you had; it's a lie to say you had not." Charlie says you should have seen Claude's face of indignation at the words. "Percy," said another of the boys, "you would fight them for saying that, if you were not a coward."

'"Of course, we all know he is a coward," said one or two voices.

'"Prove it," Claude said; and drawing himself up, stood in an attitude of defence.

'"Then you will fight at last?" said the boy.

'"Certainly not," said Claude; "but let any one try to strike me, and I shall know how to receive him."

'"Ah! a braggart as well as a coward," said the whole; and the biggest boy of the set rushed at him. In one moment he was laid level with the ground. Another and another came on, and met the same fate; the rest took alarm, and held back. The three who had attacked him rose from the ground, and sneaked off; but from that day, Charlie says, there has been no bullying of Claude, and he has become the leader of the games; and knowing that his love of peace does not arise from cowardice, but from principle, they have learned to respect him, and in some degree to follow his example.

'Now, papa, wasn't it prime? isn't it a jolly story? I think Claude is a perfect brick.'

Mr Willoughby could scarcely believe his ears, so

great was his astonishment at Frances's concluding words. 'The story itself may be a very good one,' he said; 'but the words in which you have just expressed your opinion of it, and of Claude, are so perfectly novel to me, from the lips of a young lady, that I can hardly credit having heard them aright. Miss Manley, may I ask, is Frances in the habit of using those sorts of terms?'

Miss Manley was obliged to acknowledge that for some time past she had had occasion to reprove Miss Willoughby for her way of talking.

Frances, though somewhat daunted by her father's displeasure, made her defence by saying, 'Oh, papa, there is no harm in it; you should hear the Roscoe girls speak! They say it is all the fashion for even grown ladies to speak that way; and that no one cares a bit for a girl now-a-days who can't talk slang.'

Mr Willoughby was angry now. 'Frances, listen to me. I wish no quotations of the sayings or doings of the Roscoe girls,—poor orphan girls, who have been brought up in a most careless manner, and who are more to be pitied than blamed for their faults; but I will allow no daughter of mine to use, even in jest, the phrases *you* call slang. As to there being no harm in them, I am the judge of that, and consider there is immense harm in young girls making use of language, which would be tolerated in no proper society. Perhaps you might find a few school-boys, or foolish young men, who would laugh at a girl speaking in that way, and even apply some of their slang expressions to her for doing so; but, Frances, believe me, the men and women whose opinions are at all worth the having, will never admire anything in a young girl which is calculated to make her bold and unfeminine. Be ready to meet any emergency calmly, and as self-reliantly as you like; but be assured, that in the eye of both God and man, "a meek and quiet spirit is of great price." I speak strongly, because I feel the subject an important one, and I hope it is one on which I will never have occasion to speak to you again. I am glad your mamma had gone to the nursery before you told your story, for I know she would have been much vexed to hear her daughter speaking so foolishly; and as I trust you will at once give up the practice, I shall say nothing to her about it. Now you know my commands on the subject; see they are not disobeyed.'

Frances left the room somewhat sulkily; but for all that, she felt in her own heart that her father had spoken the truth, and gave up the slang language, even in jest.

Would that all young girls would do the like, instead of following the fashion of the foolish. Believe me, that the refined and cultivated of both sexes shrink from the girl who, throwing off the gentle reserve of her nature, apes the manners and conversation of men.

Charlie Whitmore was quite right in saying that Claude now took the lead amongst his companions, and was respected by them all. His earnest endeavours to do right, his fearless declaration that his wish was to obey the will of God—all had an effect; and even those who laughed at his principles admired his conduct. Yet Claude was no model boy, too perfect to be real; only what every one may become, who, in the strength of the Lord, is seeking to walk in the narrow way. He was a quick learner, but, truth to tell, he would far sooner have been out playing cricket, or rambling about in the woods, or down amongst the rocks on the shore, than poring over Latin or Greek. 'Small use to a soldier!' he observed to Mr Marshman.

'And yet, Claude,' he replied, 'where will you find such spirited accounts of battles as in your Greek and Latin authors? Once read the original, and you will acknowledge that even the best of translations are tame.'

'Well, yes,' said Claude; 'to be sure the battles are worth reading, so I suppose I must plod away, Mr Marshman; but it's hard work,' he said, with a laugh.

A want of steady application was one of Claude's besetting sins, and one against which he had to wage a constant warfare. Let him but put his mind to the subject, and his powers of learning were quick; but often time was squandered, by a mere want of fixing his thoughts on what he had to do.

Mr Marshman pointed out to him this fault, and begged him to beware of it. 'One of the commands of the Great King to His children, Claude,' said he, 'is, "Whatsoever ye do, do it heartily, as unto the Lord;" and remember, that, without a habit of steady application, no one will ever rise to greatness or usefulness in the world. Time frittered away can never be recalled.'

Many a conflict had Claude with this foe, but with the sword of the Spirit he overcame it, and the letter which reached Colonel Percy from Mr Marshman, on the very day of his starting for the Crimea, told him that, with truth it might be said, his boy was improving in all things, 'obtaining,' the writer said, 'by the grace of God, the best of all victories—that over himself;' and as the accounts of Ada told the same story, the heart of the father was filled with joy and gratitude; he had good reason to believe that his motherless children were pressing on in their heavenly race, sustained by the hand of the Great King; and amidst the dangers which encompassed him, Colonel Percy dwelt in peace, blessed in the belief that, were death to remove him from this world, he and his children would yet meet one day, through the merits of the Lord Jesus, in the golden palace of the King of kings, from which they would go out no more.

CHAPTER XIV.

'His soul, to Him who gave it, rose;
God led it to its long repose,
Its glorious rest.
And though the warrior's sun has set,
Its light shall linger round us yet,
Bright, radiant, blest.'

THE month of September was fast drawing to an end; the fresh green of the summer foliage was changed into the glowing variegated tints of autumn, and the summer heat was exchanged for the cool fresh breezes of the advancing season.

Anxiously did every one, in those days, wait for news from the allied armies. That the landing on the Crimea had been successfully effected, was already known; but the next news, it was thought, would be of an encounter with the enemy. The first account of it which reached Willoughby House was brought by Claude.

The lamp was already lighted in the drawing-room, where the whole party were assembled, when a loud knock at the house door drew forth exclamations of wonder from the young people, as to what visitor it could be coming at that time of night, when suddenly Claude rushed in, waving his cap round his head, and calling out, 'Victory! victory! A famous battle has been fought, on the 20th of the month, on the banks of the Alma; and we have beat the Russians out and out, forced them to retreat, and leave us masters of the field. Hurrah! no soldiers like the British, say I!'

All shared his joy and excitement; even little Minnie joined in the hurrah; but Ada clung to him, and begged him to tell her if papa was safe, and if there were many killed.

He threw his arm kindly round her. 'Well, Ada dear, there have been many killed and wounded, of course. The names are not known yet, but I'm sure, somehow, papa's safe; I seem just to feel he is so. Don't fear, dear; depend upon it we will get a letter from himself soon.'

It was boyish reasoning, certainly, and comfort with a slight foundation; but, nevertheless, Ada was comforted, perhaps more by the very tone of her brother's voice than by his words. How often is it the case, that our worst fears are quieted by seeing that some one we trust in does not share them! Claude's cheerful words conveyed assurance to more than one of the party, allaying the heart-pang with which Miss Manley too had heard the news.

As soon as the excitement had calmed a little, Mr Willoughby drew from Claude an account of all he knew, and also how he had heard it. It was easily explained. An uncle of one of the boys at Mr Marshman's had come from London to see him, and had brought the news, received by telegraph late the night before. Particulars were not given, but the victory was stated to be a complete one: the French and English armies had fought together, side by side, and had succeeded, after a hard-fought battle, in routing the enemy; and now, it was supposed that they would at once press on to Sebastopol, and, if need be, besiege it. Mr Marshman had at once given Claude leave to go to his uncle's, and tell the news; desiring him to return early next morning.

With hearts filled with more than usually solemn thoughts, the little party assembled that night at evening worship. The portion of Scripture chosen was the 46th Psalm, so full of the believer's calm assurance of faith amidst all dangers. 'God is our refuge and strength, a very present help in trouble: Therefore will not we fear, though the earth be removed, and though the mountains be carried into the midst of the sea.' The concluding verse was specially fitted to comfort and sustain the anxious ones: 'The Lord of hosts is with us; the God of

Jacob is our refuge.' Mr Willoughby read also the next psalm, dwelling on the second and third verses: 'The Lord is a great King over all the earth. He shall subdue the people under us, and the nations under our feet.'

Not many days elapsed ere the anxiously looked-for letter arrived. Colonel Percy was safe. That, for some time, was all that Ada could comprehend; but Claude eagerly devoured the contents. His father had made a hurried plan of the battle-field, pointing out the different spots where his own regiment had been most hotly engaged. 'The bullets were flying thick enough, Claude,' he wrote; 'and I only wish you could have seen how bravely our soldiers fought. Many of my loved comrades have fallen fighting nobly. Young hearts, and brave, lie low, who rose that morning in the full vigour of manhood. Peace be to their memories! they rest in a soldier's grave. Ah! how many sad hearts there will be in our own beloved country, even in the midst of the joy of victory! Thanks be to the Great King, that He hath preserved me in safety, taking hold of shield and buckler, standing up for mine help. We are all eager to be on, and long to stand before the walls of Sebastopol.

'Ada would have liked to have seen some of the beautiful vineyards we passed through, shortly before the fight began. Our men pulled the grapes in handfuls, and, even when fighting, might be seen holding bunches of them in their teeth whilst they fired at the enemy. Dear children, often and often, in the very thick of the battle, your faces rose before my eyes; but I was enabled to commend you, in faith, to the King of kings. How Claude would have liked to have been by my side! and I think I hear him say, as he reads this, "Wouldn't I just!" But, truth to tell, I fear much his father's hand would scarcely have been so steady, nor his heart have beat so calmly, had he been so.

'One brave young officer, little more than a boy, fell close beside me; in his hand he bore the colours of his regiment. From one eminence, on which a breastwork had been thrown up, the enemy had been routed; and the brave boy dashed on, eager to plant his colours there. In the act of doing so, a ball struck him; he fell, even in death, grasping the crimson flag entrusted to his care. A soldier sprang forward, and, raising the colour, planted it again, claiming the spot for his regiment.

'Alas! ere now there will be heavy hearts in his Scottish home; burning tears shed, I doubt not, for the brave blithe boy. But he sleeps in Jesus; I saw something of him at Varna, and recognised in him the marks which distinguish the children of the Great King; and often have I wished, and fondly dreamed, that he and my Claude might one day be acquainted.

Not long before the battle, he said to one who knew him well: "If I fall, tell them all at home, I know that the blood of Jesus cleanseth from all sin." And now, why should we mourn that his young life, which was so bright and unclouded, should prove so short? His work is accomplished, his warfare o'er; and now he rests in the palace of the Great King, beholding the Son, through whom he overcame, face to face, where wars and rumours of wars are heard no more, but all is righteousness, and peace, and joy for evermore.

'Dear children, press on, looking unto Jesus. Soon, how soon, none can tell, may the summons come: "The Master is come, and calleth for thee."

'The Captain Ainsworth I wrote of in my last is strong again, and fought bravely, escaping untouched. Our loss is computed at nearly 2000 in killed and wounded. The French have suffered much less, some say scarce more than 1200, others believe not nearly so much. The loss sustained by the enemy is thought to be very great. I hope to write soon again. Dear children, you are ever in my thoughts; and I know how fondly you remember your loving father.'

The letter formed the principal topic of the day, and Claude found an attentive audience in his school companions, as he told them the story of the boy officer, who met his death so early, nobly fighting for Queen and country. And Arthur listened in silence to the story; and long after the others had ceased to talk of it, he sat and dreamed of the child of the Great King, who had gone from the bloody field of battle straight up to the golden palace; and the boy thought, though he said it not, that ere long he would meet him there, though the road which led to it, in his case, was from no far-off battle-field, but from his own lovely Devonshire home; and in his heart he was glad it was so, for he loved to think that his last look on earth would rest on the pleasant scenes and loved faces he held so dear. Then, one moment absent from the body, he would be present with the Lord, amid the company of redeemed ones in glory, and in the presence of God the Judge of all, and of Jesus the great Mediator.

CHAPTER XV.

'The man that looks on glass,
On it may rest his eye;
Or if he pleases, through it pass,
And hence the heavens espy.'

REALLY, Ada, I cannot allow such work to pass; it must all be picked out and done over again, and that before you go to walk. So set about it at once, and let me find it finished when I come back.' And so saying, Mrs Willoughby left the room, leaving Ada gazing at the work she held in her hand with a most disconsolate look, most unlike the pleasing bright smile usually seen on her face.

Mrs Willoughby prided herself on being a good needlewoman, not merely clever at all sorts of fancy work, but especially at useful plain work, too much despised by the ladies of the present day. She was also determined that Frances should be taught to sew well, and had always taken that department of her education on herself; and had so far succeeded, that Frances bid fair to equal, if not surpass, her mamma at her needle.

With Ada it was very different: she was far from a good worker, and had no love for it; and the sewing in the parlour, with her aunt for a teacher, was always looked forward to with dread. But this day was worse than usual, and the tears fell fast as Ada looked first at the portion of work to be done, then at the bright autumn sun shining, which seemed to invite her to come out and enjoy it.

She saw Frances and Arthur cross the park with Miss Manley, and longed to throw down her work and join them; but her task must be done, and so she worked away, although, we must confess, with a bad enough grace, and a feeling as if she were just then a very ill-used person. There were angry thoughts in her heart: the stitching was far too difficult for her; her aunt had been unjust; in short, any one was to be blamed rather than herself; and if a still small voice whispered, 'Doest thou well to be angry? the fault was all your own,' she strove hard not to hear it.

Ah! Ada, in turning away your ears from that voice, you are turning away from the voice of the Great King Himself. Rather listen, and take heed to the gently spoken admonition: the stone on which you have stumbled is offended pride, and it is a hard one to overcome; but one word of entreaty to your Guide, and at His command it will disappear.

The parlour door opened, and Ada, whose work

was now almost finished, looked up, expecting to see Mrs Willoughby, but to her surprise saw her uncle. 'Ada,' he said, 'your aunt asked me to tell you, that, as some visitors have arrived, she cannot come to you; but if your work is done, you may go to the garden, and wait there till Miss Manley and the others return from their walk.'

Ada's face expressed no joy at the permission. 'My work is not done yet, and, besides, I don't care about going to the garden to-day,' was her reply.

The tone of her voice amazed her uncle, so unlike was it to the gentle one in which she generally spoke, and, somewhat displeased, he was moving away without saying any more; but he paused ere doing so. His great desire was to act a true father's part to these children, and he asked himself, Would her own father have thus left his child without a word of warning or reproof? He drew in his chair and sat down. 'What is wrong to-day, Ada?' he said gently. 'Is the work so very difficult, or what is it?'

'Yes, it is so very difficult to do it nicely, and aunt is so hard to please,' said Ada; 'and I can't bear to sew.' And further words were stopped by tears.

'Ada,' said her uncle very gravely, 'did you try to do the work as well as you could? Did you try with all your heart? Tell me.'

No; Ada could not say she had tried much that day. She did not like sewing.

'And how about pleasing the Great King, Ada?' said Mr Willoughby. 'Do you think He is pleased with you to-day? Did you not think of trying to do your work well to please Him?'

My work! uncle; oh, no. How could my doing it well be anything to Him?'

'Ada,' replied Mr Willoughby, 'do you not know it is written, "*Whatsoever* you do, do it as to the Lord?" The most commonplace work may be, and by the child of God ought to be, done to His glory; and certainly if, instead of idling over your work, and so displeasing your aunt, and getting yourself into trouble, you had taken up your sewing, and resolved to try to do your very best (because, as a child of the Great King, every duty you have to perform you must do to Him), you would have found the fancied difficulty vanish, and have been the happy cheerful little girl you usually are.'

Ada's angry spirit was quieted now. 'I never thought,' she owned, 'of doing my work well to please the Great King, but another time I'll think of it, and I know it will help me; only it seems such a very small thing, I can scarce fancy that the Great King will care to have me to do it. Please, uncle, repeat that text again.'

'Whatsoever ye do, do it heartily, as unto the Lord.' It is in the third chapter of Colossians; and, Ada, there are some lines on the subject written nearly three hundred years ago, which you must learn some day. Here is a verse or two :

' " Teach me, my God and King,
In all things Thee to see ;
And what I do in anything,
To do it as to Thee."

And this quaint old writer, George Herbert, whose writings you will read some day, maintains, and rightly too, that

' " Who sweeps a room as for God's cause,
Makes that and the action fine." '

' Sweeps a room ! Oh, uncle ; and yet, I suppose, *whatsoever* ye do, may mean that too. Oh, I wish I had only thought of it sooner. Then perhaps I would not have displeased the King so much as I have done to-day. You don't know what very wrong feelings I had ; I was so angry.' And the child threw herself into her uncle's arms.

' Ah, Ada, you must seek the forgiveness of the Great King, pleading the merits of His Son. Had you sought His aid when you felt the wrong feelings, it would not have been refused. Remember the King's daughter must be all glorious within, made so by Him who alone can do it ; and then, but not till then, shall she enter into the King's palace.'

From that day Mrs Willoughby noticed a decided improvement in Ada's working powers ; and the sewing hour, once so much disliked, now passed pleasantly. More and more the Child of the Kingdom was learning to act on the grand Christian principle, 'Whatsoever ye do, do all to the glory of God.'

The lesson was learned, it is true, after many failures; but still it was learned; and thus, step by step, the heavenly Guide was leading on His child in the right way to the city of habitations, whose builder and maker is God.

CHAPTER XVI.

'Grief dwells in France and England
For many a noble son;
Yet louder than the sorrow,
"Thy will, O God, be done."
From desolate homes is rising
One prayer—Let carnage cease.
On friends and foes have mercy,
O Lord, and give us peace.'

DECEMBER'S snow lay thick on the ground; biting cold blew the northern wind, driving along the falling snow and sleet in the very faces of the brave men who stood for hours, by day and night, in the trenches at Sebastopol. Hard work it was, requiring a far greater amount of courage to endure, than that called forth by the hot excitement of a close conflict on the battle-field. A patient spirit, as well as a brave one, was needed to bear up against both piercing cold and cannon balls. Alas! many lives, worn out by excessive toil and exposure to the inclement weather, were lost in these winter days.

Side by side, in a scantily furnished tent, waiting for the hour to come round which was to summon them to exchange their place in the tent for one in the trenches, sat Colonel Percy and his friend Herbert Ainsworth. Both sat lost in thought. Colonel Percy had just finished a letter to Claude, and the faces of both children were vividly before his eye, the fair-haired girl and the dark noble boy; and with theirs another face was mingled, more fair, more beautiful than either—it was that of his departed wife, gentle, loving, unselfish; and as he listened to the booming cannon, and thought of the long weary hours of suspense she would have suffered on his account had she been alive, he was able to thank his God and hers that she had been spared the trial—had been taken away from the evil to come.

The thought that she was at rest in the golden city, acted on his heart as a gentle chord, inviting and drawing his thoughts from earthly to heavenly things. Above the noise of cannons' roar, and all the din of warfare, he heard the sounds of the harpers before the Throne, and the joyful song of praise of the redeemed choristers of heaven.

How near the eternal world appeared to him as he mused thus! and how narrow the space which separated him from the Church in heaven! The words of the beautiful hymn rose to his lips:

'One army of the living God,
To His commands we bow.
Part of the host have crossed the flood,
And part are crossing now

There was comfort to him in the thought. He loved at all times to realize the communion of saints; but time was passing, the hour of duty had come round. The Colonel got up, and touching the arm of his companion, who sat lost in a reverie, said, 'Come, Ainsworth, we must start for the trenches despite wind and snow.'

Herbert Ainsworth rose at once, but it took him a while to rouse himself from his dreams, and return to the work-day world around him. Not that his day-dreams had been altogether pleasant, for they were strongly mixed with remorse. One sweet loving face, with its deep blue trusting eyes, ever seemed to look at him with a glance of grave reproach, and tell him that his selfishness had blighted a bright young life, and caused deep sorrow to a heart which had loved him only too well.

Yes! now when it was too late; now, when he feared that Mary Manley had learned to despise his very name, Herbert Ainsworth awoke to the consciousness of her real worth, and of the true heroism of the heart he had wilfully thrown from him. He traced the motive of her action now to its true source, obedience to the Great King; and he himself, as yet but a beginner in the school of the heavenly Teacher, wondered at the strong faith and stronger love which enabled Mary Manley thus to deny herself, in order to do what she saw was the will of God concerning her. If his love to her had ever grown cold, it was warm enough now; and the knowledge that she still loved him would have brightened up all around him. That the fact was hid from him, was but a just retribution for his past conduct; but, even as it was, the spark of hope—which somehow would not die—that perchance she still thought of, still prayed for him, sustained and strengthened him to bear up and fight on, till, with a name renowned for brave deeds, he might claim her as his own, or at least seek and obtain forgiveness of the past. Something whispered to him, that woman's love, once given, was not lightly removed; and so, with that sweet face ever present in imagination, Herbert worked away in the trenches, and bore up unflinchingly amidst hardships, new indeed to many who underwent them all.

Brave men! how many earnest prayers were offered up on their behalf from British homes, and offered, blessed be God, not in vain; and none more earnest were uttered, than those which rose from the hearts of the children, we write of, in Willoughby House—those children of the Great King. Often in those December days, Claude, Ada, and Arthur met together, and talked of the scenes enacting at Sebastopol, and, as accounts reached them of the dreadful cold, the suffering, and the sickness which prevailed, their hearts saddened; and their very powerlessness to help, and the very strength of their pity, led them to do that which proved more powerful than any other thing they could have done—to beseech the Lord, who had all power, to arise and help, for Christ's sake.

'Ada,' said Arthur one day, 'could we not pray more for the brave soldiers than we do? Look here, see what the Great King tells us, in His Word, about the power of prayer. The Israelites were engaged, under the command of Joshua, in fighting with the men of Amalek. For long it was doubtful which side would get the victory; now one side prevailed, now another. From the top of a neighbouring hill three people watched the battle: they were Moses, Aaron, and Hur. Moses prayed to God; and when he prayed, the Israelites prevailed; when from weariness he ceased, the Amalekites prevailed; and so, as Aaron saw how tired Moses had become, he made him sit down, while he and Hur held up his hands. He prayed steadily; and Joshua and the people of Israel discomfited Amalek and his people with the edge of the sword. You see what prayer did then, Ada, and perhaps it will do so still; nay, we know for certain it will, now,' said the child reverentially, 'for Jesus has said, "Whatsoever ye shall ask in My name, I will do it."'

And so, in simple words, but in full assurance of faith, the children besought the Great King to sustain and comfort the soldiers, and give them victory over all their enemies; and their prayers ascended and mingled with those which were offered up from many a household for the same object. And the answer came; not at first, in victory and cessation of the war, but in the increasing patience and long-suffering endurance evinced by the noble army before Sebastopol, and in the bold testimony borne by many a soldier of the cross, even with his last breath, to the power of real religion to uphold under all trials, and remove the fear of death.

CHAPTER XVII.

'He who His Son, most dear and loved,
Gave up for us to die,
Shall He not all things freely give
That goodness can supply?
Behold the best, the greatest gift
Of everlasting love!
Behold the pledge of peace below,
And perfect bliss above!'

THE Christmas holidays had begun: Claude was at his uncle's; and some relations of Mrs Willoughby's, Mr and Mrs Carew, with their two young daughters and a boy about Arthur's age, had come to remain till the New Year; so the party at Willoughby House was a large and pleasant one.

A slight covering of snow lay on meadow and hill, and the frost had for some time been more severe than it usually is in the south of England; but though some might grumble at the unwonted cold, not so did the youngsters at Willoughby. Snow-balling and skating were pleasing enough for some of the party, and the exhilarating air and beautiful scenery more than satisfied the others; and all, from little toddling Minnie (who thought the snow was sugar, and insisted on tasting it), regretted when the too early setting sun recalled them home, and loved to linger as long as possible watching the glowing colours that painted the clouds, which rested on the hill-tops, and glistened on the pure white snow. And Arthur, as he gazed, fancied that right behind the floating golden clouds lay the entrance to the city where dwelt the King of Glory.

Colonel Percy's letters afforded abundant topics of conversation to the whole party. Claude never wearied of repeating the details of the noble charge at Balaklava on the 25th of October which his father had written to him, describing in glowing terms the glorious appearance of the British squadrons under the command of Lord Cardigan, as they dashed across the plain in obedience to orders, exposed as they were to the heavy fire of the enemy on all sides, and engaged in an attack which made the world wonder. Alas! alas! ere the splendid brigade returned to the lines, half its numbers lay dead on the field. 'But,' said Claude with sparkling eyes, 'they died at their post of duty; and what more glorious death can a soldier desire than to fall on the field of battle?'

In the midst of Claude's enthusiastic descriptions,

Ada's gentle voice was sometimes heard. 'Oh! Claude, but war is a dreadful thing. Think, only think of the desolation and misery which the report of that awful loss will cause to so many hearts, leaving parents childless, wives widows, and, Claude, perhaps very many children orphans.'

But Claude stoutly maintained, in spite of all that, and much as he felt for the relations of those who fell, 'Still, Ada, there must be great consolation for them, in the thought that their friends fell doing their duty, fighting for Queen and country;' and, led on by her brother's words, the next moment would find Ada listening with all attention to his account of the battle of Inkerman, telling how, in the dark foggy morning of the 5th of November, the Russians had attacked the British troops at Inkerman, and how nobly (though somewhat taken by surprise) they had fought, often carrying on the fearful struggle in a hand to hand combat; how the enemy was repulsed, then once more made a new attack; how the French army hastened to share the battle; and how for seven hours the combat continued—the carnage on both sides very great, the ground strewn with the dead; but how in the end the Russians fled in disorder. The victory was a great one, but it was gained at a fearful price.

The girl's tears fell fast as Claude spoke. The Carews had seen the Guards leave London—a noble sight—and now could only picture them as lying powerless in death, as that regiment had suffered even more than others at Inkerman, drawing from their noble commander (as Colonel Percy wrote) an expression of bitter regret that, whilst so many of his friends had perished, he should have survived, saying, 'It is not my fault if I am not amongst them;' showing, as he spoke, his clothing riddled with balls and grapeshot.

The long winter evenings were not spent in idleness, nor in mere selfish gratification round the blazing fire, in the tastefully adorned, warmly carpeted and curtained drawing-room of Willoughby House. The brave men suffering from cold and privations in the Crimea were not forgotten; and all hands were busily employed, working warm articles of dress to be sent out in a box to Colonel Percy, for distribution amongst the soldiers of his regiment. For some time, Frances, Ada, Mrs Willoughby, and Miss Manley, had been busy at the work, and a good collection of warm comforters, chest preservers, muffetees, and stockings was already finished; and as many friends had come forward and volunteered to help, the articles were increasing daily; and the children saw with delight, that a much larger box than was at first anticipated would have to be got.

Two or three times, whilst the Carews were with them, the Willoughbys invited several of the young people from the neighbourhood, and had a large working party—one of the party reading aloud some favourite book, or relating an instructive story, whilst the others plied their needles. Ada's dislike of work was overcome now, and she felt obliged to her aunt for having taught her to knit, as she was thus enabled to make many warm articles, which otherwise she could not have done. But all declared that the handiest amongst the girls was Frances; she was quite in her element, and most useful in shaping and arranging work for others. At first she had entered into the plan more as an amusement than any other thing; but as she worked on, she felt a double pleasure in the thought that she was doing something to help her fellow-creatures. Mr Hole's words were not altogether forgotten, and sometimes, in the midst of her work, she would start at finding herself inwardly repeating the words, 'Inasmuch as ye did it not to one of these My brethren, ye did it not to Me:' then, half-ashamed of thinking of these things, she would begin to hum some lively air, and hope she wasn't going to turn dreadfully good, like Ada or Arthur.

But she never mocked them now for speaking and thinking of the Great King, as she had once done; only she wished—oh, so much!—that Arthur's eyes would not look so very bright, nor his cheek have such a delicate pink hue; and sometimes the thought, that perhaps the King he loved so well would take him away to dwell with Himself, filled her with terror; for, better than father, mother, or little sister, Frances loved her gentle, clever brother. Oh no, she could not live without him; and so, refusing to entertain the idea of his being ill, she would never listen to her mother, when she spoke of her fears that Arthur's health was failing, saying, 'There is nothing the matter with him, mamma, but just moping.' But even whilst she spoke thus, her eyes filled with tears, and she would run out of the room to hide them.

Mr Willoughby watched his daughter closely, and observed the softening of her nature; and the glad hope filled his heart, that one day would see her also a child of the Great King.

Mary and Jessie Carew were two gentle, lady-like girls, about the ages of Frances and Ada. Skilful workers, they helped largely to fill the box, and never wearied of hearing Ada and Claude tell the stories of the war written home by their father. The children of religious parents, they were well taught in sacred things; but they had not yet learned, as Ada did, to realize Jesus as an ever-present guide to them. Reverently as they spoke and thought of Him, He was yet afar off, more respected as the Saviour of their parents than loved and known as their own. In close companionship with Arthur, Claude, and Ada, they could not fail to see that the motive of all their actions was love to Jesus, the Son of the Great King, of whom they loved to speak; and as they listened to their converse, new views and thoughts of Jesus dawned in their hearts. And when they both could say, in truth, ere many years had passed, that the God and Saviour of their parents was theirs also, they loved to tell, that the first time they really began to desire to know Jesus as their friend and Saviour, was during their Christmas visit to Willoughby House, when they saw how happy Ada and the boys were in the full confidence of being children of the Great King.

The party at Willoughby House was to break up on the second day of the new year, and the box was to be packed up, and sent off on the first. so there was no time to be lost; articles had to be finished, and books (which Colonel Percy had said would be very acceptable) to be got. All were therefore fully occupied, and many pleasant conversations took place whilst the hands were busy.

Arthur, when wearied with playing with Claude and Alfred Carew, would often join the working party, and take part in their talk; and some of the girls remarked, that, whatever subject they might be talking about when he joined them, ere long he led the conversation almost imperceptibly to the Son of the Great King, who came so many hundred years ago into the world, and lay, a little babe, in His mother's arms in the manger at Bethlehem. The best of all Christmas presents, he said to Ada, was surely this, God's unspeakable gift.

Amongst the contributors to the box were many of the villagers, eager to give what little help they could to the soldiers. Even blind Mrs Barnes sent some pairs of warm stockings of her own knitting, and little Willie brought a new comforter to Arthur, and asked him to send it. 'Father gave it me for myself,' said he, 'but the poor soldiers need it more than me; and so, when I asked father if I might give it them, he said yes. Please, sir, to take it, for it's the only thing I have.' The humble gift was not refused, and the offering, in the eyes of the Lord, might not have been the least costly in the box.

The box was filled and sent off. Holiday time had come to an end; and a new year had begun, on the events of which, whether sad or joyful, the blessing of the Great King was earnestly implored, and the party at Willoughby House dispersed, never all to meet again till they shall do so within the city where partings are unknown.

CHAPTER XVIII

‘ The sea, the sea, the glorious sea !
What has the earth so fair
Of hill or valley, grove or lea,
Which may with it compare ?
Oh, I could sit for hours to look
Upon its wide expanse,
And read, in its unwritten book,
Fresh charms at every glance.’

‘FRANCES, Ada, look here ! have not we been successful to-day ?’ said Claude and Arthur in a breath, as they ran towards a sheltered nook, where the girls sat, on a wooded declivity overhanging the beautiful beach at Ilfracombe ; ‘ only see !’ And they proceeded to take out of the vessels which they carried some beautiful specimens of marine animals, feathery plemose, the bright rosy anemones, one or two snowy ones, some of the graceful cave-dwellers, and two brilliantly-coloured crasses looking like dahlias.

The girls were delighted with the new additions to their aquarium, declaring, however, that the boys might keep the crasses ; for, beautiful as they were, they preferred the smaller ones ; and the large kind, at all events, were more suited to the tank.

'What lovely sea-weeds !' said Ada. 'Ah, here is a kind will do charmingly to form a group for the screen I am making for Miss Manley. How graceful they look !'

'Ah, but,' interrupted the boys, 'you should have seen them in the place they were growing ; the most beautiful little pool you can imagine, far away among the rocks yonder. This rose-coloured sea-weed fringed the whole of it with its feathery branches, just like a little fairy tree. Some of those brilliant-coloured crasses were sunning themselves in it, spread out in all their beauty ; funny little fish were darting about it : in fact, it was just a natural aquarium ; and the water so clear too. But I can tell you the very shadow of our hands, as they touched the water, changed the whole appearance of it. The fish disappeared in a moment, the crasses drew in their tentacles, and, becoming quite ugly, covered themselves with sand and channel as we tried to catch them.'

The girls declared they must see the pool for themselves the next day, but now they must go indoors, as it was dinner-time ; and starting up, the four set off towards their pleasant lodgings close by the shore.

July sunshine and warmth had brought no returning health to Arthur Willoughby, nay, rather increased his languor; and at the doctor's advice his parents had taken him and the rest of their family to try the effects of the sea air at the quiet town of Ilfracombe. They had been there for three weeks, and certainly Arthur had gained strength since they came, and thoroughly enjoyed, as did the others likewise, the rambles amongst the rocks and the pure sea breeze. Miss Manley had gone home for a short time to visit her friends; so the children were left a great deal to themselves, and spent most of the day in the open air.

News from the Crimea were still anxiously looked for. The battles of the Alma and Inkerman, and the bold charge at Balaklava, were now as household words, and yet the allied armies were still occupied in besieging Sebastopol. Long and obstinately the enemy held out, but the Allies feared not. They were confident of victory sooner or later. Colonel Percy wrote constantly now, to tell of some brave repulse given to parties of the enemy, who endeavoured, in the dead of night, to make a sortie, hoping to surprise the allied army; but finding them fully prepared, were obliged to retreat again within the walls, though often not without loss of life on both sides. Even in the midst of all the uproar of the incessant warfare, Colonel Percy told how a chosen few, officers and men, used to meet together, now in one tent, now in another, to pray and sing praises to the Great King. Some there were who at first scoffed at the little company; but as it became evident that the men who composed it were remarkable for bravery, patience, resolution, kind-heartedness, and holy lives, the derision ceased, and the mockers acknowledged that, if religion produced such fruits, it could not be such a bad thing after all.

As the children played on the beach, they often remarked a fine-looking old man, who was almost always absorbed in reading the papers, only raising his head for a moment, as the merry young voices met his ear, to look at them, and sometimes kindly to wish them good-day.

One morning Claude determined to have a talk with the old man, and find out who he was; for he had said from the first that he was sure he was an old soldier, whilst the others had stoutly maintained he must have been a sailor, he was evidently so fond of the sea. Taking for granted that his guess was the right one, Claude began his attack thus: 'That was a famous repulse our troops gave the Russians last month, was it not? You like to read about the war, don't you, sir?'

The old man's eye glistened as he replied, 'That I do, my young sir; and if this hand were not so frail, and these limbs so tottering, it's not Tom Evans would be sitting here, when his Queen and country are needing men to fight in their cause. Many and many's the battle I've fought, and none can say they saw me flinch for ball or sword. There's many a one cries out for peace, peace; but it's war for me: flashing swords, and the roar of cannon,—these are the sounds that please "old Tom," as the children call me. I'm old and grey-headed and useless now, you'll see, but I was young and strong when I fought at Waterloo under the Iron Duke. Yes, that was a battle. They may speak of Alma and Inkerman, but it's Waterloo was the battle of battles, let who will say the contrary. But the charge at Balaklava was a grand one, I'll say that: 'twas a rash order to give, may be, "Take yon guns;" but the way 'twas obeyed was grand; yes, grand,' repeated the old man, his eyes flashing fire; 'and 'tis no part of a soldier's duty to dispute commands; he has nothing to do but obey. Remember that, young sir, for you have the look of a boy who would some day be a soldier; your great duty is obedience to your commander, be he right or wrong in his orders.'

'I know that,' Claude answered boldly, 'for I am a soldier's son, and have been taught that lesson from a child.'

The old man drew from the boy an account of his father's services, regiment, and name, and waxed eloquent in his own stories of the Peninsular wars, ending by asking Claude to come to his cottage, which was close by, and see some curious coins and two medals which he had. Claude could not go that day, but promised he would soon. The old man had taken his fancy ; but he grieved to hear that he scrupled not, in talking, to take the name of God in vain.

As they parted, the old soldier repeated his boast, 'None can say Tom Evans ever in word or deed failed to obey his captain's commands.'

'And yet,' said Claude, half timidly, 'I notice you don't think much of disobeying the commands of the Great Captain.'

'The Great Captain! who is he, boy? and what do you mean by my disobeying his commands?'

'I mean the Lord Jesus,' Claude answered; 'the Captain of our salvation, whom every one of us is bound to obey, before whose judgment-seat we must all one day stand, and give in our account of how we have obeyed His orders; and He has said, "Swear not at all." Don't do it, Tom Evans, for the Lord Jesus is a good Captain, and all who fight under His banners are blessed.'

Without waiting for more words, Claude was off, eager to tell that the old man *was* a soldier, and to relate some of the stories he had told him.

The old man looked after him, muttering to himself as he did so, 'That's a strange boy; bold-like too, and yet can preach like a parson, better than some I've heard. The Great Captain—that's what he called Jesus—expects us all to obey His commands. Well, Tom Evans, you'll certainly be cashiered and shamefully expelled for disobedience to that Captain's orders, and there will be nothing but justice in the sentence either; not a word could you say in your own defence before that court; and you're old, and the time of your reckoning can't be far off. Heigh, ho! but that bit boy made me feel oddish. There's an old Bible at home, it has not been opened for many a day; but I'll have a spell at it, and see what the Captain says. I like that boy, too, I do; he's the very making of a soldier in him. And so he did not like to hear the old man swear. Well, soldiers did not mind that so much in my day; but things change, no doubt.' And the old man walked slowly home, and turned into his solitary house; for he liked to live alone, although a married daughter and her children lived only a short way off, and had pressed him to make her home his.

A well-read copy of 'Wellington's Life' lay open on the table; but that night it was the long-neglected large-printed Bible that the old man pored over, and the verse he dwelt the longest on was the third in the second chapter of 2d Timothy: 'Thou therefore endure hardness, as a good soldier of Jesus Christ.' He could not find out yet anything about the Captain of salvation; but he had found out one thing, and that not a small one, that he was *not* a good soldier of Jesus Christ. The way of salvation was all dark and unknown to him: through a long lifetime he had dwelt in that darkness, and knew not that it was not light; but the reflected light of a child of the Great King had shown him the darkness which surrounded him, and the old man started as he saw how thick it was.

Some days passed ere Claude visited the old soldier in his humble cottage. The welcome he received was a hearty one, and it was plainly with no small pleasure that the old man showed off his stock of curiosities, and poured into the boy's ears one story after another of his youthful days and adventures. Ere Claude rose to go, the soldier pointed to the large Bible on the table, saying, 'Young sir, I've been taking a read at that book, looking to find out what orders the Great Captain you spoke of has given to His soldiers; and it's plain to me, when the hour of reckoning or the day of inspection comes round, that Tom Evans stands a poor chance: no way of escape for him, either, that I can see.' Yet the old man looked anxiously at the boy as he spoke, as if hoping he might contradict his assertion.

'Oh yes,' said Claude eagerly, 'there is a way of escape for all who confess their sins and seek forgiveness. Look here,' and Claude opened the Bible, 'it is written, "The blood of Jesus Christ cleanseth us from all sin;" and again in the first chapter of Ephesians we read, " God hath accepted us in the Beloved (that's Christ), in whom we have redemption through His blood, the forgiveness of sins." The way of salvation is plain enough, Tom. " Believe on the Lord Jesus Christ, and you shall be saved." The great Captain is worthy of our love. When nothing but certain destruction awaited every one of us, He gave His life to save us ; so, surely, He has a claim on our love, obedience, and gratitude, has He not ?'

' That He has, sir, and no mistake ; but it's the enemy I fear, that Satan : he'll be always tempting me to disobey the Captain, and not fight under His banners ; and, you see, it's with shame I say it, but all my life I see, now, it's under Satan's banners Tom Evans has fought, and it will be hard work to escape out of his hands.'

' True enough, Tom,' said Claude, ' but, as my father told me, Christ is stronger than Satan ; ask Him to help you, and fight your enemy for you, and He'll do it : never fear, only trust in Him. It is written, " Resist the devil, and he will flee from you." You must read about the Christian's armour, in which all the soldiers of Christ must be clothed. Here is the place, in the sixth chapter of Ephesians. See, we are told we must put on the whole armour of God, that we may be able to stand against the wiles of the devil.'

The old man read the passage carefully, and mused

over it long after Claude had left the cottage, saying to himself as he read, 'Well, it's plain enough that the battle's a hard one, and the enemy very strong and very crafty, but then the Great Captain is stronger than Satan; and, as the boy said, they that are with us are greater than all that are against us.'

The old man's progress in the knowledge of divine things was slow; but through the darkness the true light had shone, and would go on increasing to the eternal day; and, even at the eleventh hour, the old soldier would join the band, who, through much tribulation and many difficulties, yet with a secret strength and joy of which the world knows not, are pursuing their way under the guidance of the Son to the palace of the Great King.

The month of September found the Willoughbys and the Percys once more in their lovely home, revelling in the beauties of country scenery at this season, when the silent processes of nature during long months have reached their consummation, and have covered the earth with fruit, while the trees stand as yet with their summer beauty untouched, awaiting the breath of autumn to clothe them with a beauty pleasing to look on, though betokening decay.

On a day of more than ordinary loveliness, when the earth was covered with the bounty of the Lord, the glad news spread from county to county in the United Kingdom that Sebastopol was taken. British arms had once more, by the blessing of God, proved successful; the war had ceased, the oppressed were free. The nation hailed the news with unbounded joy. Peals of cannon sounded over the land, telling of victory; bells rung out the glad tidings, brilliant fireworks proclaimed the universal joy, and from many a church rose the strain of grateful praise to Him who had given the victory, and once more gave the prospects of peace. A sense of repose and rest descended that night on many a heart, that, for long weary months, had beat in restless anxiety for loved ones amid the dangers of war.

At Willoughby House the news were received with a joy almost too deep for words; even Claude's warlike spirit rejoicing at the thoughts of a peace (gained by victory) which would once more restore their father to them. But it was in the quiet of her own room that Ada gave vent to her feelings, and then it was in adoring prayer to the Great King, who had preserved their father safe, and made the war to cease. The party that evening was joined by Mr Hole, who came to congratulate the Percys on the good news, and unite with them in returning thanks to the Great King for His mercy, each one saying from his heart, even as David did of old, 'Blessed be the Lord God of Israel, our Father, for ever and ever.' 'Thine, O Lord, is the greatness, and the power, and the glory, and the victory, and the majesty: for all that is in the heaven and in the earth is Thine; Thine is the kingdom, O Lord, and Thou art exalted as head over all;' each one seeking that the time might soon come when men should 'beat their swords into ploughshares, and their spears into pruning-hooks, and nation shall not lift up sword against nation, neither shall they learn war any more.'

CHAPTER XIX.

'The merry homes of England!
Around their hearths by night,
What gladsome looks of household love
Meet in the ruddy light!'

SOFT spring breezes were blowing; delicate green leaves covered the trees, quivering as if in the exquisite enjoyment of life; and the bright sunbeams played on the rosy blossoms of the lovely Devonshire orchards, ere Colonel Percy found himself in Willoughby House, and once more clasped his children in his arms, the weary months of toil, and danger, and separation, all forgotten in the joy of reunion.

In the end his arrival was unexpected; the party were assembled in the drawing-room, music and the merry laughter of children filled the room, drowning the sound of carriage-wheels, when the door opened, and Colonel Percy stood in the midst of them. One glance, and with a shout of joy his children were in his arms.

A warm welcome from all greeted him; and as he

sat on the sofa, his arms encircling his children, his heart was filled with true happiness. Even whilst answering the questions addressed to him on all sides, his eyes rested with delight on his boy and girl, noting the change and improvement which nearly two years had made on their appearance, and observing, with an eye sharpened by parental affection, the expression of countenance which told him of mental and spiritual growth. In Ada's he read a character strengthened and ennobled by her love to God and man, and rendered more self-reliant, since he had seen her, by the circumstances in which she had been placed. And in Claude's he read the same bold, eager spirit as of old; but the firm set of mouth, and whole expression of face, betokened a temper more held in subjection, a mind more concentrated, than of old.

Ada said little, and only those who knew her well would have known how happy she was; but to them her peaceful, loving, grateful look spoke volumes. Not hers the nature which finds vent for its happiness in words; no, although happiness pervaded even the very depths of her heart, its outward expression spoke more by the eyes than the lips. But Claude's joy was expressed more openly, and, but for deference to the feelings of others, would have found vent in a true schoolboy's hurrah

A pause in the conversation let him put the question, 'Please, papa, will you tell us something about the taking of Sebastopol on the glorious 8th of September?' The request was granted, and a short account of the assault given.

'For hours the struggle, Claude, was a hard one, and at times victory seemed doubtful; once masters of the Malakoff, we knew Sebastopol must fall. Many a brave man perished ere that was achieved; but when it was so, shouts of triumph told we felt that victory was now ours.

'During the night, loud explosions and blazing flames told that the enemy had abandoned the town, blowing up their defences, their powder magazines, and different establishments, and setting fire to the city. Morning confirmed the truth of our suppositions; the Russians, under the leadership of Prince Gortschakoff, had departed, having destroyed everything they could, and sunk a number of the ships in the harbour, leaving the allied armies conquerors. You can scarcely imagine the desolate appearance which the once fine town bore when our troops entered it; scenes of horror on every side, smouldering ruins, crumbling houses, and dead bodies of men and animals.

'Yes, Claude, the glitter of war is only at a distance: those who have witnessed the many horrors attendant on even a short campaign, must acknowledge it to be a necessary evil; and even the most heroic and boldest of soldiers should look forward with rejoicing to the time when nations shall not learn war any more.

As Colonel Percy spoke, his eye rested on Arthur, who sat with his large dreamy eyes fixed on his uncle, apparently absorbed in listening to him; yet with the appearance of one whose thoughts had been led by the conversation to things beyond and above. Something in the look struck Colonel Percy, and he saw with pain the boy's very delicate appearance. Laying his hand kindly on his shoulder, he drew him nearer to him. 'Well, Arthur, what are you thinking of?' he said, somewhat playfully. 'Did you not like to hear my description of all those horrors?'

Half-bashfully the child said, 'No, no, it was not that; I liked to hear: only you made me think of some words, and they led my thoughts to other things.'

'What were the words, Arthur?' said Claude; 'do tell us.'

Gently he whispered, '"They shall not hurt nor destroy in all My holy mountain, saith the Lord;" and I was just thinking how pleasant it would be to be there, "for the people who dwell there shall be forgiven their iniquities."'

The boy's words were so plainly the simple expression of his real feelings, that Colonel Percy felt much attracted to him: he saw with regret the sad look which crossed his father's face as he regarded his child, whose whole appearance now indicated only too plainly that ere long the place which now knew him would know him no more for ever.

Not till the children were alone with their father, holding sweet converse, as of old, did Ada realize how happy she was. Together they spoke of the Great King, and, kneeling at the throne of grace with grateful hearts, rendered thanks to Him for having preserved them, and brought them again together in safety; and as Ada lay in bed that night, she thought of the last time she had received her father's good-night kiss, and, remembering her dream, acknowledged that, in very truth, the Son of the King had upheld her weak steps, had overcome the many obstacles and thorns which had at first encompassed her way, and was, she doubted not, leading her onwards to the palace where He dwelt.

Very calmly she slept that night, no bloody battle-fields before her eyes, as had so often been in the past months; only her father's figure, and, clearer far than of late, the face of her gentle mother, peaceful and sweet as of old; so life-like, that when the bright sunshine roused her from her slumber, ere she fully awoke to consciousness, and only aware that some very joyful event had occurred, it was some minutes ere she could divest herself of the idea that not only her father, but her mother also, were waiting for her morning kiss. But the truth soon shone clearly; not on earth would she again see her angel mother, or kneel at her knee in prayer. No, that meeting would take place in far fairer scenes, even in the City of Light, in the presence of the Great King; till then, in dreams only would she behold the so loved face.

But that did not damp the joy she felt in once more waking to the delight of knowing that her father waited impatiently her morning salutation; so bed was left with a bound. And her Bible-reading was not a lonely one that day; for, just as she had seated herself to commence it, Colonel Percy entered, and, seating himself beside her, read of the Lamb who stood on the mount Sion, having with Him the hundred and forty and four thousand redeemed ones who have His Father's name written in their foreheads.

'Those, Ada,' he said, 'were all children of the Great King; no mistaking them for such even on earth, for the seal was on their foreheads, and "holiness to the Lord" was engraved thereon; known to all around them as followers of the Lamb, not merely by bearing His name, but as being a peculiar people, zealous of good works; and now, when we read of them in glory, they are singing a song of praise before the throne, which they only can sing who have learned it on earth.'

'Papa,' said Ada, looking up into the clear blue sky, 'mamma is there singing that song, is she not?'

'Yes, my child, in full assurance of faith, we can

say she is : she learned that song on earth, we know; and now she is, without fault, before the throne of God, washed in the blood of the Lamb, and one of the happy ones who follow Him whithersoever He goeth. Ada, even if we could, would we bring her back to earth, to lean on our frail love once more?'

For some minutes, gazing upwards in solemn thought, then with a smile playing on her lips, as if she had caught a glimpse within the veil, she said, 'No, papa, she is better, far better so. One day we shall see her again, and never part. Papa, I hope that you and I, Claude, Arthur, Frances, uncle, aunt, and dear little Minnie, all will be there.'

'God grant it, Ada; within the palace of the Great King may we all meet, no member lost, a family in heaven.'

CHAPTER XX.

'He led them forth by a right way, that they might go to a city of habitation.'—Ps. cvii. 7.

VERY pleasant were the summer weeks which Colonel Percy spent with his children at Willoughby House. Time seemed to fly on wings; all were delighted with the Colonel's pleasant, winning manners, and turned to him for advice in perplexity, or sympathy in pleasure. Now he might be seen superintending farming matters in company with Mr Willoughby; then ready at Mrs Willoughby's desire to make some calls in the neighbourhood, on people anxious to see one who had gone through the dangers of the Crimean war. Not only his own children, but Frances and Arthur also sought him in any difficulty, and got him to be a partaker in their pleasures.

Kind and courteous to Miss Manley, grateful for the trouble she had taken with his girl, he yet little suspected how interested the governess felt in him, as the friend of Herbert Ainsworth; and with what breathless delight she listened, when in conversation he mentioned his name as one of the bravest of officers.

But not for much longer was the gentle spirit of Mary Manley to be so sorely tried. When Colonel Percy had been about a month at Willoughby House, the post brought two letters, in Herbert Ainsworth's handwriting, the one to Colonel Percy, the other to Miss Manley. In the one he told his friend the story of his love, making full confession of the part which he had acted, and of the nobler Christian way in which Miss Manley had behaved. To Miss Manley he wrote only a few lines, telling how bitterly he had repented of the step he had taken, and how deeply and fondly he still loved her. More he did not feel himself privileged to write, till he was assured of her forgiveness, and had obtained her consent to see her. 'Only write one word of permission; only say you have not learned to forget me as I deserve,' he wrote, 'and a few hours will find me by your side.'

Such was the strain of the letter, which in one moment made Mary Manley's heart beat more joyfully than it had done for many a day. It may be that a stronger-minded woman would have rejected the lover who had once cast her off, and, even whilst inwardly suffering herself, would have rejoiced in her revenge. But Mary Manley was strong-minded only in some things: strong in doing right;

strong in denying herself rather than turn aside from the path of duty; but as for quenching her deep affections, and now that she had the power of glorying in being able to say to her former lover, 'As you once thought you could do without me, I will not forgive you now,'—as for writing a lie, and saying she had ceased to love,—unheroic as she may seem, she could not do so, not she. Like a very woman as she was, and a simple loving one too, she laid down her head and cried over the letter; then took up her pen, and, after asking counsel only of the best Counsellor, and of her own heart, she wrote the words, 'Come, Herbert, I forgive all,' and kneeling in prayer, thanked the Great King for granting her such unlooked-for bliss.

'Well, I declare,' said Frances (when some days afterwards her uncle was relating the noble way in which Miss Manley had acted), 'Miss Manley is quite a heroine after all; only you know, uncle, I think she certainly should have refused to see him again, instead of looking, oh, so bright and happy, and consenting, mamma says, to be married to him soon too. She should, at least, have put him off for some time till she had proved him; that's what I should have done.' And the girl drew herself up in the conscious dignity of nearly sixteen years.

Colonel Percy smiled at her words and air of determination. 'Wait a bit, Frances, till you are tried, and perhaps your fine theories will all be swept away by the flood of a real pure, forgiving love, which erases past offences in its course, and makes them seem as though they had never existed.'

Ere long a new governess filled Miss Manley's place, and the autumn months saw the latter the wife of Herbert Ainsworth, united to him in spirit as she had never formerly been; for now they were, in Christ Jesus, members of the little flock whose King dwelleth in heaven, and who appointeth for each of His children the place and the trials on earth which will prepare them best for the place assigned to them in the kingdom above.

Miss Manley's departure was a real grief to Ada and Arthur, though her successor, Miss Williams, was one well qualified to fill her place, and perhaps better suited for the charge of a girl of the age and temperament of Frances.

All too soon the time of Colonel Percy's leave of absence sped away, and Ada learned, somewhat to her surprise, that though his regiment was to be stationed, probably for some time, in Ireland, she was still to remain an inmate of Willoughby House. Indeed, no other plan was feasible, unless that of placing her at a boarding-school in Dublin, which was once thought of, where her father could often see her. But much as he would have liked the plan, he soon saw that the best one would be to allow Ada to remain, for some time at least, under the charge of her uncle and aunt.

Fond as Ada was of all at Willoughby, she heard her father's determination with a sad heart. Once more a separation was before her, and this time not only from her father, but from Claude also, who, after the Christmas holidays, was to go to a military school at a far distance. But she showed her disappointment as little as possible, lest she should grieve the kind friends who, she knew, had arranged all for what they believed her good. Claude was the only one who saw how cast down she was, and they talked over the subject together; and he pointed out to her some bright spots in the scheme, which cheered her not a little.

'Only think, Ada,' said he, 'how sorry Arthur would be if you went; see how he likes to have you sit beside him and talk to him, and what pleasure he takes in reading all the queer old stories, just to have the pleasure of telling them to you. And Frances, too— only this morning she came rushing to me with such a bright face, to tell me it was now quite fixed that you would remain; "and Claude," she said, "to tell you the truth, I am as glad as glad can be; I could not bear now to be without Ada."'

Well, Ada was glad to hear that; though Frances and she were very good friends now, still she did not fancy she cared much about her. Oh, she knew by and by that she would see it was all right, only now she could not bear to think of it; 'alone, without even you, Claude, near.' But her brother had cheered her, and she must not seem to rebel against her father's wishes; and as she re-entered the drawing-room, with a face not so bright as usual, it is true, but still not sad, the kind loving looks which welcomed her told that all knew and sympathized with her disappointment, and were pleased to see how bravely she bore it. Keenly her father watched her. For her good he had acted, but the pang he felt was as sharp as hers.

'Ada,' he said, as he wished her good night, 'the Son of the Great King has promised to lead His people, who put their trust in Him, safely to the palace; but He has said that He must choose the way. Sometimes He leads them away from the smooth road, which they would like to tread, and takes them by a rough crooked way, but, for all that, the right one for them.'

Ada thought of her dream, saying, 'Well, papa, I am glad He chooses for me; I could not have chosen this one for myself.'

CHAPTER XXI.

'I know not the way I am going,
  But well do I know my Guide:
With a childlike trust I give my hand
  To the mighty Friend by my side.
The only thing I say to Him
  As He takes it, is, Hold it fast;
Suffer me not to lose my way,
  But lead me safe at last.'

ADA'S visits to the blind widow were still regularly paid; the old woman waiting impatiently as the usual hour for her visit came round, her quick ear ever the first to catch the sound of the light footstep she loved so well.

For some weeks Ada, at Mrs Barnes' request, had been engaged in reading aloud to her the 'Pilgrim's Progress,' the old woman taking in the different scenes so clearly, just as if she saw them all, and meditating on them during the long hours of the, to her, dark day. The day after her future plans had been fixed, Ada, with a step not so light, and a far heavier heart than of old, set off to the village, across the lovely meadows, and through the shady flowery lanes, the gentle breezes just moving the leaves, and playing softly on her forehead.

She was to read that day of Christian and Faithful, pilgrims to the better land, arriving at a beautiful river, on the banks of which were green trees, bearing all manner of beautiful fruit; and beyond the river, on either side, was a lovely meadow, beautiful with lilies, and ever green. For some time the pilgrims loved to rest there, drinking of the pure water and eating the pleasant fruits; and Ada, as she looked back on the three months which her father had spent with them, felt as if she, during that time, had been resting by just such another river of pleasure, and now, like the pilgrims, was but little disposed to turn away from it, and press on again, through perhaps many dangers, to her home.

She read to the old woman how the pilgrims, as they went on, saw the pleasant path by the river-side come to an end, and a rough rugged one take its place, and how they were afraid of it, and shrank back; but seeing a pleasant path leading away through a green meadow, how they chose it, and walked therein, though they had been told to follow the road which lay straight before them, and turn not aside; how the path, which looked so fair to the eye, led them straight into the dominion of Giant Despair, who seized them, and carried them off into Doubting Castle, and there beat and cruelly treated them, till they were almost dead, and were delivered at last only by the magical power of prayer and faith.

As Ada read these things her voice trembled; and Mrs Barnes, having heard that Colonel Percy was to go away, divined the cause. She laid her hand on the girl's head. 'Take heart,' she said, 'never you fear. The Great King is telling you to leave the pleasant river-side a bit, and choose the rugged path; but He'll hold you up in the way, and brighten it up for you. See, it was because the pilgrims turned away from the path before them, that they got into such trouble. Don't you do that, dear young Miss, but just keep right on till you reach the palace.'

Yes, Ada saw that was the best, the only way for a child of the Great King. Anything, any sorrow, was surely better than going astray, and falling into the hands of Giant Despair. So, with a lightened heart, Ada went home, her own soul watered whilst she had been watering others; and meeting her papa with Frances and Claude, set off for a country ramble, and returned laden with wild flowers and fruit, little Minnie bounding to meet them in order to run off with some of the flowers for Arthur, who lay on a couch, weak and weary, only the eye very bright, and the spirit very loving.

Willie Barnes was at school now; but once a week

he came up to the house to read his lesson to Arthur, whose failing strength hindered him from getting often to the village, save now and then to the house of God. But the sweet, childish voice, whose notes once sounded so sweetly there, was scarcely heard now; and Mr Willoughby, and even his fond mother, were beginning to realize how frail was the thread which held their darling only boy to earth.

One bright autumn day, Arthur lay on his couch close by the window, looking, as he loved to do, at the beautiful tints of green and gold, and watching the light clouds which flitted across the sky, obscuring every now and then the rays of the sun, and casting momentary shadows on the earth. Colonel Percy, who sat talking to him, observed with deep compassion the troubled look in Frances' face, as she sat busied with her work, her back half-turned to Arthur, that he might not see her face; for in very truth her young heart was sorely troubled. Only that morning her father had told her the doctor's opinion, that Arthur's strength was fast failing: all remedies had failed; all that could now be done was patiently to watch and smooth his way home.

Impetuously Frances ran away from her father, refusing to believe what he said. She said she knew that doctors were almost always wrong—liked to make the worst of all things; and she knew Arthur was not very ill, only he had a bad cough, and that made him so breathless when he tried to walk. Oh, he just needed somebody to cheer him ; she would go and take her work beside him, and rouse him up a bit. And this was the way she did it : she came humming into the room, meaning to begin a joke with him, when something in his face, a look of calm peace, as of one whose thoughts were far above earthly things, struck her with dismay, and told her that the doctor was right. She tried to speak, but a ball seemed to rise in her throat as if it would choke her ; so she pulled in her seat, turning, as we have seen, her back to her brother, and worked on, her breast heaving with suppressed emotion.

She was relieved when her uncle came into the room, and Arthur began to talk to him. 'Tell me again,' he said, 'about the young boy officer you wrote of, who fell at Alma, who was a child of the Great King. His journey was not a long one, but mine will be far shorter; different ways, but the same ending, and the same guide, the Son of the Great King. Uncle, you know Ada's dream ; I always felt my journey would be short, and now I can see the palace gate, with the bright light quite close, and I am so glad.'

His words were cut short by a loud sob from Frances, as she dashed her work on the floor, and rushing out of the room, threw herself on her bed, and sobbed as if her heart would break.

Colonel Percy rose at once, and sending Ada to sit with Arthur, followed Frances to her room, anxious to comfort her. Waiting till the violence of her grief was over, he said kindly, 'Dear Frances, is the knowledge of Arthur's danger so new to you? Did no one warn you?'

She broke in on his speech, but not with the impetuous voice as of old. 'Yes, oh yes, papa did, and mamma also; but I would not believe it, would not believe that the Great King he loves so well could be so cruel, so unjust, as to take him away from every one he loves. Oh, I could not believe it.'

Colonel Percy repeated her words: 'Cruel and unjust! Nay, Frances, say not, think not so. In very love and mercy does the Great King deal with all His children, and very lovingly has He dealt with dear Arthur. His short life has been full of happiness, his mind so formed as to have tasted the purest enjoyment from all the beauties of nature, in the midst of which he has lived; and latterly the greatest of all joys has been granted to him, for the love of Jesus has filled his heart. And now, when God sees fit to withdraw him from this world, He has removed all fear of death far from him; not one fear, not one gloomy thought concerning it has crossed his mind. He thinks of it (as, indeed, it is to all who love Jesus) as only a going home; and dearly as he loves you all, he loves Jesus more, and is longing to depart and be with Him. Oh, Frances, when God has thus so tenderly drawn him to Himself by the bands of love, can you say that He is cruel any longer? Can you not rather return Him thanks, from your inmost heart, for His loving-kindness towards him, and pray that to the end He may continue it, making Arthur's heart long more, day after day, for the hour when he shall behold Him face to face?'

The girl's sobbing ceased as she listened to her uncle's words. In her heart she confessed their truth, and, for the first time, a real longing desire filled her heart, that she too could say that she was indeed a child of that merciful, loving King. On the last day Arthur would stand on the right hand, but she feared that her place would be on the left. Mr Hole's words sounded again in her ears; she must seek forgiveness through the blood of Jesus now, if she would not hear Him then say, 'Depart from Me.' The dew of the Spirit had roused to life the seed which had lain so long dormant, and the cry of the girl's heart was, 'Bless me also, even me, O Lord;' and ere Colonel Percy left to join his regiment, as he shook hands with Mr Willoughby, he was able to say, 'I hope, and expect to hear from you soon, that Frances too has joined the band, and wears the badge of the children of the Great King. But even though the blessing tarry, wait for it; it will surely come. She is a child of prayer, and we know that ours is the sure promise, " Ask, and ye shall have."'

Yes, so it was : God, in His own way, was guiding the spirit of the girl to the cross of Jesus, where she would find both pardon and strength ; but the guide he had commissioned to lead her was a little child, whom, after that work was done, and that labour of love fulfilled, He was to take to Himself, to receive the crown of glory prepared for him in heaven.

CHAPTER XXII.

'My Father's house on high,
  Home of my soul, how near,
At times, to faith's far-seeing eye,
  Thy golden gates appear!
Ah! then my spirit faints,
  To reach the land I love;
The bright inheritance of saints,
  Jerusalem above.'

A FIRE burned brightly in the neat little drawing-room of the parsonage at Ashton; a lamp on the centre table shed a pleasant, subdued light around, shining on the pure white china tea-cups, bright new silver tea-pot, and a pretty bronze tea-kettle, as they stood ranged before a gentle-looking young lady, who busied herself in preparing tea, whilst casting every now and then anxious looks towards the door, as if expecting some one to enter.

Presently she started up with a smile of welcome, as the door opened, and her husband, the young clergyman, Mr Hole, entered. He looked fagged and worn out; but the hearty welcome he received, the warm fire, and, let us add, the good cup of tea he drank, cheered him up, and ere long made him look like himself again.

Not for long had the parsonage been inhabited by the pretty little blithe woman he now called wife. Only one short month before, when November winds were blowing, and dead leaves whirled through the air, bringing a feeling of desolation into many hearts, the bells of the little village church rang out a merry peal, and the band of school children in their Sunday best, and a few of the still lingering flowers of autumn in their hands, stood ready, in their own rustic fashion, to welcome the clergyman and his young bride to their home; and from that day, in the eyes of the happy husband, there seemed to be perpetual sunshine in the parsonage. November winds or December snow all vanished, or at least were forgotten, in the presence of his bright young bride.

But on the evening we write of he looked more worn out than his wife had yet seen him. He had gone out after an early dinner, and had only just returned when it was almost eight o'clock. He had ridden some way to baptize a child, and see some old people, who, owing to the great distance, rarely could get to church; and then, as he had promised Mr Willoughby, he had called at the house and remained some time.

'And how was Arthur to-night?' said his wife; 'not worse, I hope?'

'No, I think not, no marked change; the doctors say, only a gradual loss of strength. But many an advanced Christian might learn a lesson from that child; his heart glows with love to Jesus, and love to all around him; his faith so simple, yet so strong; his patient unselfishness so remarkable. No wonder that the thought of losing him is a sore trial to parents and all of them. But the child truly has not lived in vain; he has done a great work in his home. The mother, kind and hospitable as she has always been, is only now, it seems to me, fully awaking to the saving knowledge of the truth, learning to know Jesus as a loving personal friend, and becoming willing to let the child she loves so well depart and be with Him.

'And Frances, too, is changed—wonderfully changed. She has by nature a bold temper, and, young as she was, a year ago was learning to scoff at holy things; but now she is much softened. Her greatest pleasure consists in sitting beside her brother, listening to him or reading to him. As I went into the room quietly with Mr Willoughby, we heard Arthur say to his sister (whilst a large screen hid us from sight), "Dear Frances, Jesus wishes you so much to come to Him. Oh! taste and see that the Lord is good; blessed are they who put their trust in Him." And the girl answered, "Yes, Arthur, I *have* tasted and found it, only it is more fear than love with me yet; but I believe the love will come one day." The conversation ceased as we walked forward, and Arthur greeted me, as he always does, with his happy smile.

'As I walked home, I have been meditating on the wonderful way in which God deals with His children; and how apparently simple, and often lowly, are the means He makes use of to work out the counsels of His will. Step by step I have marked the change in that household, from the mere outward form of religion to the living spirit. First it was the sweet little Ada Percy whom He commissioned to speak to son and father of the way of salvation. Then it is the dying child He has permitted to be the instrument of drawing the hearts of mother and sister to the cross. Truly God hath chosen the foolish things of the world to confound the wise, and the weak things of the world to confound the things which are mighty, that, as it is written, "he that glorieth, let him glory in the Lord."'

Yes, all that Mr Hole told his wife that night was true; Arthur Willoughby's illness was proving a blessing indeed to all around him. Life went on much as usual in his home: the girls were a great deal in the schoolroom busied with lessons; the daily walks were taken as usual; but somehow Arthur's spirit pervaded all. The lessons were done more heartily, that they might get down sooner to sit with him; the walks were brightened by the search after some particular fossil, or stone, or plant, for Arthur.

In many ways Ada's Christian, kindly spirit showed itself. Dearly as she loved Arthur, she was always ready to yield up her place to Frances, knowing how she liked to spend her spare minutes with him; and one day, having found a pebble which she knew would please Arthur, she gave it to Frances to give to him, knowing she liked to do so. Frances noticed it all, and sought, by increased gentleness towards her cousin, to show she appreciated her kindness.

The fruit of the Spirit, the distinguishing badge of the King's children, is Love. Tell us not of a faith which is without it, which worketh not by it. The faith which lays hold of Jesus as its object, shows its reality by the fruits of holiness. Very truly has St James declared that faith without works is dead. Nay, such a thing is not faith at all, but a mere delusion of Satan. The children of the Great King, knowing what Jesus has done in order to secure their salvation, must, out of love and gratitude to Him, and because He has saved them, glorify His name by their works.

Arthur's love to Claude continued unabated, and the Saturday afternoons were anxiously looked forward to. It was a strange sight to see these two together: the one so full of life and spirit, eager to run the race before him, yet looking up to heaven for guidance; the other, though several years his junior, having almost already reached the end of his short pilgrimage, dwelling on the very confines of the land of Beulah, getting each day nearer glimpses of the celestial city, learning, from the bright messengers that come from thence to visit him, the very language of the sanctuary, only waiting for the summons to be given, 'Come up hither.' These visits were good for Claude, good for the strengthening of his faith, ere he went forth to take his part in the world of a large public school.

One day the boys talked of Claude's departure, which was very near, and of the trials he would be exposed to. 'Perhaps,' said Arthur, 'you will find it hard work to confess the Son of the King there; but, Claude, you won't draw back; you won't, I know. You won't be ashamed of Him; from yonder sky I'll watch you, one of the cloud of witnesses, and I know I'll not see you draw back, for God will strengthen you.' Presently he said, 'Please, Claude, read to me; read about Paul proclaiming his faith in God, and giving thanks to Him, as he took bread before all the crew of the heathen ship. It must have been difficult, perhaps dangerous, for him to do it there, but he did it. Claude, shall I give you a motto?'

'Yes, oh yes, Arthur, do,' said Claude.

'Well, here it is. Wear it like a ring round your finger. "God, whose I am, and whom I serve."'

Claude repeated the words, and inwardly prayed that, come what might, and be in what company he might, he would never be ashamed to confess that motto, and act as a servant of his Master in heaven. Often, often, in after years, when tempted on all sides to forget and deny his Lord, did that motto rise to his remembrance, and with it the soul-speaking eyes of his dying cousin, as he said, 'You won't, I know you won't be ashamed of Jesus;' and once and again strength from above was granted him to confess boldly his allegiance to the Great King. So, being dead, Arthur yet spake.

The whole party were assembled round Arthur's couch one clear frosty December night, when Mr Willoughby put into Claude's hand a letter addressed to him in a strange, unformed handwriting, which had come in the forenoon, but which he had forgotten to deliver. Claude wondered greatly at the quaint appearance of the letter, and knew of no one who wrote like that. At last, after a good deal of wonderment, he opened it, and read :—

'HONOURED SIR,—My father, Tom Evans, died here last night, and this is how he bade me write to you. "Tell the young gentleman," he said, "the

Colonel's son, that the old soldier has fought his last battle; and, no thanks to himself, nor because he deserved it in anywise, he is going to a home above, purchased for him, and prepared all ready by the Captain of his salvation. Glory be to His great name! And," said he, "tell the young master he has no fear about the great day of inspection now, for the Captain has promised to answer for him, and forgive him all the sin of having once fought under the banner of the enemy; and as the Captain is Himself to be Judge, Tom Evans fears no longer. Thank," he said, "the gentleman for having told me, even at the eleventh hour, of the great Captain of salvation, and bid him hold fast unto the end, fight the good fight of faith, laying hold of eternal life; and, through the great Captain, he'll be sure to come in conqueror at the end. The blessing of an old man be on his head."

'That, honoured sir, is what he bade me say; then he began to repeat, half aloud, words that a soldier friend had said to him the day before,—

"Then I'll march up the heavenly street,
And pile my arms at Jesus' feet."

And just after that he looked right up, saying, "That's the tattoo, I must away"—and the spirit fled.'

As Claude ceased reading, every eye was moist

with tears. Mr Willoughby pressed Claude's hand, saying, 'Thank God, my boy, for having made you the instrument of leading the old man to his Saviour.' Claude said nothing just then; but, for all that, his heart was full of gratitude for having been so honoured.

'Poor old man, so he is dead,' said some of the children; 'how sorry his daughter will be!'

'She should not sorrow too much, I think,' said Arthur; 'for, you know, her old father must be so happy in the palace of the King, and will wait for her to meet him there. Oh, she must not grieve for him.'

Mr and Mrs Willoughby exchanged looks; well they knew that their boy thought of them, and hoped they would not grieve too much when the King took him away

CHAPTER XXIII.

'The struggle was o'er, the valley past
Which to him had nought of gloom;
For a ray from heaven's bright portals beamed
To lighten his path to the tomb.
He heard the sound of the angels' harps,
As he passed up the golden street;
But *his* place was before the Saviour's throne,
For there His redeemed ones meet.'

THE faint light of a March morning was beginning to struggle in the eastern sky, scarcely having chased away the shades of the long night sufficiently to lighten up the earth, which still remained lightly wrapped in the grey weird-like clothing of night, when little Willie Barnes quietly opened the door of his grandmother's cottage, and, shutting it after him, ran out through the little garden to the road in front.

He looked around him not guiltily (for, early as it was, Willie's father knew of his errand, and had given him permission), but Willie was amused at the scene around him, everything was so still. The inmates of the houses were mostly up, it is true, and stirring in-doors, but only here and there a figure was to be seen setting off to the morning work. The smoke from some of the cottages was just beginning lazily to ascend; and, finding it impossible as yet to rise up through the thick mist, it contented itself by curling into every curious form, and hanging low over the houses. But Willie passed on, down by the parsonage, past the little white gate which led to it, wondering where Mr Hole was going to so early, as he saw him cross a field right in front of the parsonage, and take the road to Willoughby House.

But Willie's road lay in the opposite direction; so he ran on, till, after crossing a meadow, the grass of which was already assuming the fresh green hue of spring, he turned aside to a well-known sheltered yet sunny nook, where the earliest spring flowers were ever to be found. He glanced around a moment, a sweet perfume was wafted close to him by the quiet breeze, and with a cry of delight the child descried, at the root of a still leafless tree, the first wild violets of the season.

'I'm glad, so glad,' he said to himself; 'I wanted them so much for him; those which grow here are always so sweet and fresh, and who knows if dear Master Willoughby will ever see another spring? Least that's what grandmother says, though I can't believe it, even though I am sure he's fit to be an angel in heaven, and looks one too, all except the wings; but he'll get them soon enough, and fly away from us. Oh, me! oh, me! and he so kind! I can't bear to have him go.'

The violets were soon gathered, the morning dew still resting on them, and Willie set off homewards, from thence to haste away to Willoughby House with his offering of love.

The sun had risen, and slowly dissipated the mist from the earth. The sun shone forth in all his brightness, foretelling a glorious spring day. How various were the feelings with which that sun-rising (like many another) was witnessed! To some it spoke of happiness and joy, dark days passed away; spring, gladness, and mirth come again. To others it spoke of yet another day of long, weary suffering and toil to be borne; and to some it spoke of suffering finishing, of heavenly rest beginning.

Thus it spoke to one of the children of the Great King. Yes, the end was now close at hand. Ere that sun arose again, Arthur Willoughby would be a dweller in the land which needeth not its rays, because of the light which proceedeth from the Lamb of God. Father, mother, sister, cousin, were around him now, tears falling softly, very softly, lest they should mar the peace of the dying boy.

Not a shade of fear on his brow; joy lighted up the clear bright eye, bright even in death. 'Father, mother, meet me there,' he said; 'dear Frances, and Minnie too, remember, all come. Jesus says, Come. Ada, the Guide is holding me fast; the light shines so bright, it keeps away all the dark. Oh! it is so beautiful, so very beautiful!' The child lay still and quiet; then 'Open the window,' he said, 'dear papa; I do so love to look out at the beautiful budding trees and glorious sun.'

Just then Mr Hole entered. 'Arthur,' he said, 'is not this a lovely day?' 'Yes,' he replied, 'my last on earth. Is it not kind in the Great King to send such a one?' The clergyman stooped over the boy, saying softly, 'Happy boy, so soon to see the King in His beauty, and the land that is afar off!'

Arthur drew his father and mother near him. 'Papa, mamma, say that you are willing that I should go; that you won't grieve too much for me. Say it, do say it.'

Ah! it was hard to do—the mother's stifled sob told how hard; the father's quivering lips also. But Mr Willoughby spoke at last the words, 'Thy will be done.' The mother, Frances, and Ada, all slowly echoed them. The child's face was radiant with joy as he heard them, and those near heard him whisper, 'Come now, Lord Jesus, come quickly.'

Just then a low knock was heard at the door, and Willie Barnes entered, his violets in his hand. As he saw the assembled party, he drew back in dismay, and would have turned and ran off; but Mr Willoughby signed to him to come in and give the flowers. Arthur raised his eyes as he entered, and faintly whispered, 'Thank you; oh, what beauties! Willie, I'm going; meet me in the palace.'

The boy stood amazed. Was this death? He had thought of it as something fearful and gloomy, but joy was written in that dying face. 'Sing,' he said; and with faltering voices they sang his favourite song, 'I lay my sins on Jesus,' finishing with the words—

'I long to be with Jesus amid the heavenly throng,
To sing with saints His praises, to learn the angels' song.'

As it finished, Arthur looked quickly up: 'I see, I see the gate of the palace opening; I come, I come!' And, absent from the body, the spirit of a child of the Great King had entered into the palace, to dwell there for ever.

Over the scene which followed we will draw a veil. Few, ah! how few, there are who cannot draw from experience that scene, too solemn, too sacred to be dwelt on. Blessed be He who by His own tears hath given to Christian mourners the sanction to weep, and yet amidst that weeping bids them rejoice, saying, 'Thy brother shall rise again!'

The body of the child lay, beautiful in death, Willie's violets in his hand; spring flowers, plucked by loving hands and wet with tears, were scattered round him;

round the fair pale forehead the eye of faith could read the words, 'Of such is the kingdom of heaven.'

Loved and loving in his life, he was not unmourned at his death. Sobs, loud and unrestrained, broke from Claude's breast as he read that Arthur was dead. What heeded he then, that some scoffing eyes witnessed the first outburst of his grief? He should see his gentle cousin no more on earth. That thought at first banished all others; then came the remembrance, 'He is with Jesus in the golden city.' That calmed the grief, and let the first ray of comfort in. And as Colonel Percy read, in the quiet of his own room, the father's account of the death of his only son, brave soldier, strong-minded man as he was, a tear fell on the page.

Who shall condemn him? who say such a tear was unmanly?

> Go search the foremost ranks,
> In danger's dark career,
> Be sure the hand most daring there
> Has wiped away a tear.'

CHAPTER XXIV.

'Easy indeed it were to reach
  A mansion in the courts above,
If swelling words and fluent speech
  Might serve instead of faith and love.
But none shall gain the blissful place,
  Or God's unclouded glory see,
Who talks of free and sovereign grace,
  Unless that grace has made him free.'

SUMMER sunshine filled a tastefully furnished drawing-room in a pretty villa residence, not many miles from London. The windows of the room opened out on a beautifully laid out flower garden, gay with all the flowers of the season, their fragrance pervading the room, as the windows were thrown open to admit the balmy air.

Seated on a low chair, work in hand, was Ada Percy. Five years have elapsed since she, along with her uncle, aunt, and cousins, had knelt by Arthur's dying bed. Those years have changed the girl into the woman; the hair golden as of yore, and the eye soft and loving. Girlish she looked still, despite her twenty years; but her character was well formed, and her manners, though winning, were marked by the gentle dignity of the woman. For three years she had lived with her father and his widowed sister, whose husband had died in India, and who, at her brother's request when he left the army, had come to reside with him, and be a companion to his young daughter.

Step by step had Ada advanced in the knowledge and practice of heavenly things. The simple faith of her childhood was still retained; her Saviour still remained to her as a friend and guide; on she was ever pressing towards the goal. The trials and troubles of daily life lay lightly on her, for she carried them all to her Saviour, and asked His counsel concerning them. The great end of life was ever present to her, not self-gratification, but the glorifying of her God in all things. She was a very sunbeam in her home; and many a time, as Colonel Percy watched her gentle, loving ways, the image of her mother rose before him, and he owned that his greatest ambition for his daughter was fulfilled in her resemblance, not only in face, but in mind also, to her he had so fondly loved.

In her own neighbourhood Ada was a universal favourite; 'so obliging, so courteous,' said her young companions; 'so staid, and with so much common sense,' said the elder ladies; whilst the verdict of the gentleman part of the community was, 'No nonsense about her, so unaffected, and yet so blithe and pleasant.' And let any stranger visit the cottages near her residence, and they would have found the favourite theme was Miss Percy : 'So kind she is, so good too, reads the Bible most as well as the parson ; and as for tending the sick, speak of that lady Miss Nightingale, don't believe she's half so good at it as Miss Percy.'

Yet Ada was no perfect being : struggles between right and wrong, betwixt duty and inclination, she had daily, as we all have ; only every day she was growing in grace, every day the desire for conformity to the image of Christ was increasing, and, a child of the Great King, she was ever seeking that in her, and by her, His name should be magnified. She did not hide the light given her from above under a bushel, but let it shine brightly around, so leading others to the Sun of Righteousness, whose light she reflected.

On the day we write of, as she sat alone in the drawing-room, her father came in with an open letter in his hand. She rose quickly up. 'From Claude, papa ?'

'No, but from his commanding officer,' replied Colonel Percy. 'Read ; it is a letter which father or sister may well be proud of. The writer is my old friend Stewart.'

Ada took the letter eagerly, and read. The writer

was great in praise of Claude, who had now been for three years in the regiment of which Stewart was colonel, stationed in India. 'I have observed him closely during that time,' he wrote, 'and have been much pleased with him in all things. His bravery as a soldier was shown in the bold way he acted, when he first joined, in an unexpected attack made by some of the hill tribes. He has the right stuff for a soldier in him; and, Percy, what I admire above all things in his character is his moral courage. No lukewarm servant is he of the Great Master; no, bold and uncompromising he stands out, never ashamed, even amidst much ridicule and sneering, to confess that he is on the Lord's side, a soldier of the Cross. Yet with most of us he is a great favourite; his open, generous, cheerful nature attracts even those to him who cannot comprehend his strong religious feelings. "'Pon my word," said a young officer in my hearing the other day, "if Percy's a common specimen of a Christian man, I should not care supposing there were lots more of them, nor even if I were to turn that sort of thing myself. Capital fellow, no doubt of that, though he does sing psalms." Such is the universal character he has gained, and I know you will be gratified to hear it; it is a good thing when Christians, by their consistent conduct, constrain even the enemies to godliness to acknowledge that there is a beauty in holiness.'

Ada's eyes were filled with tears of joy as she laid down the letter. 'Oh, papa, I am so glad; not that I doubted it, but it is so pleasant to hear it from such a man as Colonel Stewart. Claude is indeed a brother to be proud of.'

'Well, Ada,' said Colonel Percy, 'let us thank God for it. By His grace, he, as well as ourselves, stand fast. Now is our time of training and preparation for eternity; now is the time in which we can bear witness for our Lord. Our King is absent for a while, waiting till the kingdoms of this world shall have become His also; gone away but to return again, leaving His children to testify of Him boldly to all around, till He shall see of the travail of His soul, and return in glory, bringing His saints with Him. We must send this letter to Willoughby House; they will like to read it. Dear Arthur, how he loved Claude!'

'Yes, papa,' said Ada, 'and I believe the remembrance of Arthur, and his full confiding faith, has helped Claude in many a difficulty. He told me so once, and how he often thought of Arthur's motto, "God, whose I am, and whom I serve." Dear Arthur, he has not lived in vain.'

One glance at Willoughby House ere our story ends. Changes are there, but pleasant ones. Mr and Mrs Willoughby are united in a bond stronger now than ever; for, to the love which had ever existed, there is now added the everlasting bond of union in Jesus, which not even death can sever. That bond was drawn, in its closest tie, over the grave of their first-born son. Minnie, now a merry child of some ten years, is the youngest no longer. A bright little rosy boy of four years, dear little Gerald, is to be seen following his father about everywhere, bold and independent, as Arthur had never been. With deep gratitude his parents had received him as a gift from God sent to fill up Arthur's vacant place; 'perhaps,' said his father, 'another plant to rear for the heavenly garden: shall we call him Arthur?' They consulted, but by mutual agreement they said no; that name could not now be associated with the living to them; it was sacred to the dead, or rather to the redeemed one, now in glory—in the palace of the Great King.

And Frances, what of her? Ask strangers, and they might still tell you that she had grown up a bold woman, too bold by far, holding strong opinions on all subjects, and scrupling not to express them fully; scarcely feminine, it was said. But see her, if her eye rested on a boy of about nine years of age, more especially if he had large soft blue eyes; the boldness disappeared, and a gentle softness took its place, as, with a sweet smile, she would allure the child to her side, and ere long gain his confidence and love. Alone with such, be they children of rich or poor, she would tell them of a dear boy she had loved so well, whose greatest wish had ever been to do the will of the Great King, and who was now with Him above.

Yes, Frances Willoughby was indeed become a child of the Great King, not a Mary, loving to sit at the Saviour's feet, so much as a Martha, active and bustling; helpful, especially, as a leading hand in the working society of the parish, and also in many ways where a clear head and good judgment were required. Not hers, Ada's gentle, loving ways; not hers, the voice to soothe the dying bed; but let us not forget that there are diversities of gifts, but the same Spirit. The body is not one member, but many: the eye cannot say unto the hand, 'I have no need of thee;' nor the head to the feet, 'I have no need of you.' Various are the characters, different the gifts and attainments, of the children of the Great King; but in one thing they are all alike. Love to Jesus dwells in their hearts, and in some degree His image is reflected in every face. In the world, they are not of the world; called from darkness to light, they show forth the praises of Him who has so called them.

Dear readers, have you joined this heavenly band? They and they only are the happy ones. Safe for time and for eternity, their work and delight is to do the will of the Great King. That little band may seem poor and lowly, even despised now: but they are all glorious within; and ere long, clothed in the snow-white linen of Jesus' righteousness, they shall enter the King's palace, and behold Him in His beauty, and know even as they are known.

Even as when He tarried on earth, the Son of the King is this day saying, 'Come.' Turn not away from that invitation, but, just as you are, go and join the band, saying, 'Here am I, Lord; take me, even me.'

> 'And then, if any one should say,
> What's the news? what's the news?
> Oh, tell them you've begun to pray;
> That's the news, that's the news:
> That you have joined the conquering band
> And now with joy, at God's command,
> Are marching to the better land;
> That's the news, that's the news.'

THE END.

CPSIA information can be obtained
at www.ICGtesting.com
Printed in the USA
LVHW111637170422
716440LV00006B/615

9 783752 589863